'And I'm ⟨...⟩ the rest of t⟨...⟩ an option f⟨...⟩ Ben offered, ⟨...⟩ ⟨...⟩oice was shrieking ⟨...⟩ings inside his head.

He'd already grown far too close to this little family, and staying any longer was a bad idea, but he couldn't in all conscience leave her to be buried under that mountain of responsibilities again—at least, not until she'd found someone reliable to take over from him.

The look of relief and pleasure that spread over her face was like the sun coming up in the dark places inside him. But it also made his misgivings cast deeper shadows.

Kat was an incredibly strong woman, and as for her boys… What was it about Kat Leeman that had started to melt the block of ice around his heart?

Dear Reader

I'm a member of a big family that's growing larger with every year…brothers, sisters, nephews, nieces, in-laws. Sometimes the sheer numbers at a family get-together can be overwhelming, but the other side of the coin is the knowledge that there will always be plenty of people willing to help if one of us is in trouble.

Kat isn't so lucky. She's all alone and desperately needs help as she tries to cope single-handedly with her two boys and a busy family practice.

Ben certainly can't be the answer to her dreams because, on his own admission, he won't be around for long. Ever since he lost his wife he hasn't been able to settle anywhere for long, and will only promise to stay for three months. Except time doesn't seem to matter when Kat's heart recognises that he is everything she needs. And when her younger son is diagnosed with a life-threatening illness, Ben can't help but show how much he cares—discovering that he needs Kat and her boys every bit as much as they need him.

I hope you enjoy seeing how the two of them heal each other's broken hearts and become the family they all need.

Happy reading!

Josie

PS I hope you notice Mr Khan, the oh, so handsome orthopaedic surgeon who comes to visit Kat. He has a completely different family dilemma, and he's not certain whether his new colleague, Lily, is going to make things worse or better. Find out about the two of them in my next book, **Sheikh Surgeon: Surprise Bride**, coming next month from Mills & Boon® Medical Romance™

A FAMILY TO COME HOME TO

BY

JOSIE METCALFE

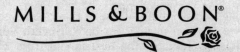

MILLS & BOON®

All the characters in this book have no existence outside the imagination
of the author, and have no relation whatsoever to anyone bearing the
same name or names. They are not even distantly inspired by any
individual known or unknown to the author, and all the incidents are
pure invention.

First published in Great Britain 2006
Paperback edition 2007
Harlequin Mills & Boon Limited,
Eton House, 18-24 Paradise Road, Richmond, Surrey TW9 1SR

© Josie Metcalfe 2006

ISBN-13: 978 0 263 85220 2
ISBN-10:   0 263 85220 2

Set in Times Roman 10½ on 13 pt
03-0207-51078

Printed and bound in Spain
by Litografia Rosés, S.A., Barcelona

Josie Metcalfe lives in Cornwall with her long-suffering husband. They have four children. When she was an army brat, frequently on the move, books became the only friends that came with her wherever she went. Now that she writes them herself she is making new friends, and hates saying goodbye at the end of a book—but there are always more characters in her head, clamouring for attention until she can't wait to tell their stories.

Recent titles by the same author:

A VERY SPECIAL PROPOSAL
HER LONGED-FOR FAMILY*
HIS LONGED-FOR BABY*
HIS UNEXPECTED CHILD*

The ffrench Doctors

CHAPTER ONE

'HE'S here!' the voice in her ear said with an unexpected touch of excitement.

Kat stifled a grin when she heard the attempt at a confidential whisper, glad that her receptionist couldn't see her amusement on the other end of the phone. Obviously, the candidate in question was standing nearby and had somehow impressed her... By his manners? By his good looks?

Well, manners and good looks were all very well, she thought as she straightened her shoulders, ready for yet another waste of time, but they weren't what she was looking for in the GP she needed to share the burden.

'Then you'd better show him in, Rose,' she suggested, hoping her weary tone wasn't too obvious.

How many interviews had she conducted so far? She'd lost count. She supposed she should be grateful that she'd had people willing to apply, but this prospective locum was unlikely to be any more interested in the position than any of the others, not when he found out exactly how dire her situation was.

A brisk tap at the door snapped her into professional mode and she forced herself to stretch her mouth into some semblance of a welcoming smile.

'Come in!' she called, expecting to see Rose's beaming motherly face as she led the man in. Instead, there was the man himself, tall, almost gaunt with the most sombre expression she'd ever seen. *So it hadn't been his charm that had bowled Rose over*, she thought inconsequentially.

'Your receptionist said to tell you that she had to stay to deal with the O'Gormans,' he reported in an unexpectedly husky voice as he stepped into the room and closed the door.

For just a second Kat nearly asked him to leave it open, the air around her feeling strangely charged by his presence and making it hard to catch her breath.

'Please, take a seat, Dr…' She gestured towards the chair that her patients usually used, horrified to find that she'd completely forgotten the man's name.

'Ross. Benjamin,' he supplied, then looked straight at her and met her gaze for the first time. 'But I usually answer to Ben.'

He's got green eyes! she thought in amazement, the colour almost unearthly when they weren't being shadowed by his thick dark lashes. One dark eyebrow rose and she realised with a swift surge of colour that she'd actually been staring at him.

'Well, then, ah, Dr Ross…Dr…ah, Ben…' she stumbled, trying frantically to get her thoughts back on track.

'Just stick to Ben. It's easier,' he said quietly, but the hand knotted around a copy of the practice's brief prospectus Rose must have given him belied his apparent calm.

'Ben,' she echoed, conscious that it felt strangely intimate to use a diminutive of his name so soon after meeting him. 'How much do you know about the situation here at Ditchling?'

'If you mean, have I seen any adverts, then, no, I haven't

because I wasn't really looking for a job,' he admitted bluntly. 'I heard that you were looking for help through a friend…of your husband's?' he ended on a questioning note.

'It could be,' she said quietly, quelling the stab of pain that came with the memories. 'Richard died of leukaemia almost a year ago, just three weeks after he was diagnosed. He never went into remission.'

She wondered at the flash of agony she glimpsed in those extraordinary eyes before he shuttered them behind a screen of thick dark lashes.

'I take it the two of you were partners in the practice?' he asked, his voice huskier than ever. 'Have you been trying to cope by yourself since then?'

Trying and failing, said a morose voice inside her head, but she refused to pay it any attention.

'With the help of one arrogant potential partner and subsequent intermittent locums,' she admitted, then, when she saw his frown, explained a little further. 'The potential partner had just finished his GP training in a big city practice and, in spite of the fact that he was still as green as grass, thought that he was going to take over as the principle partner purely on the basis that he was a member of the *superior* sex.'

Ben winced and she almost allowed herself to smile.

'Since then, I've found it a problem to interest anyone wanting a partnership to work the hours I need. Most of them complain that it would be too restrictive for either their family life, if they were married, or their social life, if they were single.'

'And the locums?' he prompted.

'Are expensive,' she returned immediately. 'Sometimes I just don't have any option, but…' Kat shrugged, remembering the most recent spell of essential cover with an inward wince. It would be months before she could afford to take any time off at that sort of rate. But if Ben looked even halfway interested…

'So,' she began briskly, suddenly remembering that it was her responsibility to conduct the interview, and that meant asking questions, 'what made you decide to move to the West Country? Have you got family in the region, or are you bringing your family with you to settle down here?'

'No family joining me,' he said crisply, the topic clearly not up for discussion. 'And it's a part of the country I haven't visited before.'

Kat's heart sank at the realisation that he was unlikely to want to stay in the practice long—what single man would? There really weren't very many options for meeting women in this quiet little backwater. But even as she silently berated herself for getting her hopes up, she was telling herself to look on the bright side. If she could persuade him to stay a while, on an associate's salary, it would give her some time to recoup and look for someone permanent.

She bit the bullet.

'So, if your references are acceptable, how long were you thinking of staying?' she asked, her fingers crossed out of sight as she wagered with herself. Even a month would be a help. More than that would be a bonus.

'If we say a fortnight,' he began, and she was hard-pressed not to moan aloud. It was hardly worth going to the effort of all the form-filling for that. 'In that time, we would each be able to decide whether we work together well,' he continued calmly. 'If not, I would leave at the end of the fortnight.'

'And if we did?' She was actually holding her breath as

she waited for his answer, surprised just how much it suddenly meant to her.

'If we work well together, I would definitely stay for three months and perhaps extend it to six,' he suggested. 'I don't usually stay much longer than that.'

She almost asked why, but the closed expression on his face didn't invite personal questions. Anyway, the last thing she wanted to do was put him off before he'd even accepted the job by sounding nosy. There would be plenty of time to find out more about him if he decided to stay on.

The phone on her desk rang, startling her.

'Excuse me,' she said with a distracted smile as she reached for it. 'Yes, Rose?'

'Josh and Sam are here,' the motherly woman announced. 'They came home on the bus. Something about Sam forgetting his kit for sports club tonight.'

Kat glanced at her watch and groaned. The boys were supposed to have stayed on at school that day, allowing her to schedule a longer clinic and tack on the interview with Dr...with *Ben* at the end. Instead, they'd come straight home at the end of classes to collect the kit needed for the after-school club and now she'd have to drive them all the way back.

'I'm so sorry,' she said as she began a frantic tidying of her desk, quickly shutting down the computer and stowing everything movable into her desk or the top drawer of the filing cabinet and locking both. 'This is one of the problems that keeps sending everything pear-shaped. Forgetful children.'

'Rose's or yours?' Ben had risen to his feet as soon as she had but it had been so long since anyone had shown her that old-fashioned politeness that it made her feel flustered.

'Oh, definitely mine,' she grumbled as she retrieved her handbag from the bottom drawer.

'Who's *he*?' demanded Josh with all the disdain that an eleven-year-old could manage when they emerged into the reception area.

'Manners, Joshua,' Kat reminded him softly, her heart aching for the turmoil her elder son was going through with the loss of his precious father. Unfortunately, those who told her it would get easier with time were wrong. Josh seemed to be getting worse by the week.

'Well, who *is* he?' Josh reiterated belligerently, somehow recognising that Ben was something more than just another patient. At least he couldn't possibly know how conscious she was of the man's quiet presence behind her.

'These are my two sons, Josh and Sam,' Kat said, holding on to her temper by a thread, sure that it would be an easier task if only she'd had more than five hours' sleep a night for the past year. 'And this gentleman has come here for an interview.'

'An interview to work here?' Sam clarified, her formerly happy-go-lucky eight-year-old asked, now needing everything to be precise and ordered in his mind. 'So you're a doctor, like Dad was.'

'Exactly,' Ben responded, with the first real smile Kat had seen, albeit a small one. 'Your mother wants to be able to spend more time with the two of you, so she needs me to take over some of the practice duties.'

Josh's scowl had grown even darker at the mention of his father and Kat knew he wasn't in any mood to give Ben the benefit of the doubt. Sure enough, before she could even draw breath to head him off, he was issuing the challenge.

'But *you* wouldn't want to work here because there's nowhere interesting to go and nothing exciting to do. You could work in a hospital.'

'I could do,' Ben agreed thoughtfully. 'In fact, I have in the past, but I wanted…I needed a change.'

Kat wondered at the change of emphasis in that word, but it certainly wasn't something she could question with her antagonistic son looking on.

'Anyway,' Ben continued with a fleeting glance in Kat's direction, 'your mother and I have agreed that I'll come for two weeks, just so she can have a bit of a rest and catch up with herself.'

Kat blinked but held her tongue. As far as she could remember, she hadn't actually had the time to go as far as offering him the job, but he'd certainly read her situation exactly…

'Mum, we're going to be late for sports club if we don't go now,' Sam interrupted.

'Sam…' It was a warning. She knew he needed his life to run to schedule, but that was no excuse for rudeness.

'Oh, sorry!' Her youngest ducked his head in apology. 'I'm sorry for interrupting, but…' He was almost hopping from foot to foot.

'Here you are, then,' Kat said as she separated the front door keys from the rest of the bunch and held them out to him. 'Go out to the house and get your kit. I'll meet you at the car. Don't…run,' she finished with a despairing roll of her eyes as he thundered out of the room and out of sight. She winced when the front door slammed behind him.

'Are you sure you don't want to change your mind?' she offered. 'It could be a very noisy two weeks living with us.'

That got more of a reaction out of him than almost anything else she'd said.

'Living with you?' he repeated faintly, clearly taken aback.

'Accommodation provided?' she reminded him. 'The practice is a purpose-built extension on the bungalow the other side of that wall and your part is in the roof conversion—a self-contained little flatlet... Well, that's a bit of a generous description,' she rattled on, unable to meet the searing green eyes comfortably while she was thinking about this man living...sleeping...showering...and all just above her head. 'There's a bedroom and *en suite* and the other room has a rudimentary kitchen in one corner, but you're welcome to join us for meals. The other locums did sometimes,' she added with a weak attempt at nonchalance when he started looking every bit as uncomfortable as she felt.

Don't let it change his mind about staying, she prayed, and was suddenly shocked to realise that it wasn't just for the sake of the practice. There was something about this quiet man that told her he'd been...*wounded*, and she felt a sudden urgent need to...to what? Heal him?

'Do you want me to lock up when I go, or would you prefer me to wait until you get back?' Rose interrupted, before she could laugh at her ridiculous thoughts, and Kat could have hugged her.

'You might as well lock up and go home as soon as you've finished with the files,' Kat said with a smile, then turned to the silent man behind her. 'At least it's only a morning surgery tomorrow, so I should have time to show you all the intricacies of Ditchling's finest...Ditchling's *only* GP surgery.' A stray thought leapt into her head and she turned back to Rose. 'Was there any problem with the O'Gormans?'

'None at all,' Rose said airily, before giving an evil cackle. 'I just threatened to sit on them if they didn't behave.'

Kat couldn't help laughing, too. Rose's diet-resistant shape would be enough to strike fear into the rowdiest of pre-schoolers, even if they arrived in groups of four.

'Right, well, I'd better get going or Sam will be old enough to drive the car himself by the time I get out there.' Kat waved farewell and set off for the door, all too aware that she had an eleven-year-old thundercloud following her, one who had been glowering almost non-stop at Ben even before she'd introduced them.

She sighed heavily, hoping she hadn't just made a monumental mistake. Hiring Ben was supposed to make her life easier, not more stressful.

'I should be back in about fifteen minutes,' she said as she pressed the key fob to unlock the car. 'If you don't mind waiting, I'll get you a set of keys and show you where everything is when I get back—unless you'd rather have Rose get them for you and settle yourself?'

'I'll wait,' he said decisively. 'There'll probably be questions that only you can answer.'

'Fine,' Kat said briefly, managing to limit herself to a single word this time and sliding into the car. If Sam didn't arrive soon, she'd be making a complete idiot of herself, babbling non-stop. She switched the engine on then glanced into the rear-view mirror to check that Josh had put his seat belt on, before turning her head and starting to reverse out of her parking space in front of the practice.

Out of the corner of her eye she saw the briefest flash of something moving before Josh shouted out and something thumped against the car. Something hard.

'Oh, God, oh, God, oh, God!' she wailed as she slammed on the brakes and flung her door open. 'Sam!' she shrieked as she leapt out of the car and sped towards the back.

'Mum…I'm sorry! I forgot!' wailed her youngest as he threw himself into her arms.

'Sam!' Relief that he was apparently totally unharmed took all the starch out of her knees and they nearly buckled.

'I forgot about going round the front of the car where you can see me,' he said urgently. 'It's all my fault.'

'Well, you'll remember next time,' she consoled him, wiping an uncharacteristic tear from a cheek that still retained a trace of childish chubbiness. All too soon he would be grown up and… She shuddered at the realisation that his whole future could have been wiped out in that split second.

'At least you weren't hurt, so—'

'But *he* was!' wailed Sam. 'And it's *my* fault!'

'*He?*' Kat glanced up sharply. 'Who?'

'I think he means me,' said a voice somewhere at the back of her car, and her knees completely gave out.

'Ben?' She was reduced to crawling on her hands and knees but she didn't have to go far to find him, his long legs out of her sight under the chassis while his upper body lay spread-eagled on the ground in front of her. 'Oh, God, *Ben!* Are you hurt? Oh, that's a stupid question! You wouldn't be lying there if you weren't. How *badly* are you hurt?'

Without even realising how she'd got there, she was at his head, her fingers gently winnowing through the thick dark strands as she searched for bleeding, lumps or, God forbid, depressed fractures. It certainly wasn't the time to notice the sprinkle of silver strands at his temples.

'Where did I hit you?' she asked as she worked her way down his neck, conscious of the strong musculature even as she was examining each vertebra for damage or misalignment. 'How did you fall?'

'My leg,' he said through gritted teeth. 'I realised you were going to hit it and tried to get out of the way but…' He shook his head in spite of her attempts to hold it still. 'I managed to stop my head from hitting the ground.'

'Is your leg broken?' Her hands were shaking now as she continued her assessment with his arms, not daring to examine the rest of his spine while his lower half was restricted by the vehicle. She didn't have enough people around to log-roll him.

'If not, it's the worst dislocation I've ever—Agh!' His attempt at moving it must have been agony but he'd closed his mouth on the curse when Sam had crouched down beside them. Kat was immeasurably touched.

'It was my fault, Mum,' he hiccuped. 'I was right behind the car and he… Is he going to die?' The words were almost hysterical and she suddenly realised just how traumatic this was for a child who had lost his father only a year ago.

'I'm too grumpy to die,' Ben volunteered suddenly, and when Sam gazed at him in surprise, he aimed an exaggerated scowl at her son. 'And I'll get grumpier and grumpier the longer I'm lying on the ground.'

'Kat! Oh, my stars!' exclaimed Rose. 'Josh came in to get me. Do you want me to phone for an ambulance?'

'No!' It was Ben who answered first. 'No ambulance.'

'But, Ben…' she protested. It was obvious he needed expert help.

He hardly gave her time to speak before he was pushing

himself up onto his elbows and beginning to inch himself backwards, out from under her car.

'It's not serious enough to warrant tying up an ambulance,' he declared decisively. 'Drive your car forward again, then you'll have room to strap my legs together for support…if Rose will fetch some bandages?' He threw a quick smile in the receptionist's direction but if he'd looked gaunt before, now he looked ghastly. His skin was pasty and had a waxen sheen and the muscles in his jaw were bulging as he gritted his teeth to brace himself for the next few inches of progress across the tiny car park.

'You will give me a lift to the hospital, won't you?' he asked, almost as an afterthought.

Of course she would give him a lift to the hospital if he was so stubborn as to refuse the offer of an ambulance. After all, it was her fault that he'd been injured. If she hadn't been distracted with her thoughts about the way he'd almost shanghaied her into giving him the job, she would have been more vigilant.

'Yes. Of course I'll give you a lift,' she said crossly. 'Just stay still until I've moved the car. You could be doing yourself more damage like that.' She turned to get into the car and saw her two sons staring down at the injured man with very different expressions on their faces.

Sam's was easy to read—a mixture of terror that he was going to watch another man dying, the way his father had, and guilt that it could have been his thoughtlessness that had caused the injury. Josh's was more complicated, most of it hidden behind the mask of impassive resignation he'd worn since his father had died, but she was almost certain she could see a measure of respect for the man's stoicism.

'Sam, you had better get in the car,' she ordered briskly.

'Get in the front and put the belt on. Josh, can you wait beside Ben? I'm going to need your help to get him in the car and then you can look after him on the way to hospital. Can you do that for me?'

For the first time in nearly a year there was a crack in his impassivity, the sudden glimpse of fear swiftly replaced by pride that she'd asked him to do this and determination that he wouldn't fail her. 'No problemo,' he said with a shrug full of the nonchalance of youth. 'And if you need some pieces of wood for splinting, Sam could get some of the off-cuts left over from when the fence was mended last week.'

'Good idea,' she said with a smile for both of them, while a secret doubt struck her.

Had she been going about things the wrong way this last year? she wondered as she quickly pulled the car close to the building again. Had she been wrapping her sons in cotton wool and giving them too much time to brood on all the ways their lives had changed for ever, rather than keeping their minds occupied?

Children's emotions were such a minefield. There certainly wasn't any way to practise helping them to cope with the loss of a parent. All she could do was take it day by day.

Kat climbed back out of the car and got her first look at the extent of the damage she'd caused.

She felt sick.

There wasn't any blood that she could see—Ben's neatly pressed suit trousers were virtually unscathed. But the shape of the injured leg was a different matter, the damage to the bones just below his knee obvious even from a distance. A classic example of a motorcyclist's fracture.

'Here you are, Kat,' Rose said, as she bustled out with a small stack of towels and several wide bandages tucked under one arm, the other fully occupied with the oxygen cylinder she'd grabbed from the corner of Kat's surgery. 'I've attached the mask so all you have to do is turn the knob to regulate the flow.'

'Entonox?' Ben's expression lightened slightly at the thought, even though his eyes were clouded with pain as they met hers.

'Unfortunately not,' she said with a grimace. 'You'd need the ambulance for that… But it should be less painful once I've got your leg immobilised. Do you want me to get you some analgesic?'

'No, thanks,' he said with a definite shudder. 'I hate the feeling of being out of control.'

'Well, I'm sorry about that, but from now on I'm in charge so you'll just have to lie still,' she said firmly. 'Now, Josh, can you put my jacket under his head to make him more comfortable, then keep him still, OK? And, Josh, you have my permission to sit on him if you have to.'

Just before she looked down to focus on the task of completing her examination and stabilising the fractured leg against Ben's sound one, she registered a flash of mischievous glee in her son's face that had been missing for far too long. What a shame that it had taken something this dreadful to bring it back.

'Here,' Ben said, offering her a wickedly sharp blade already extended from the penknife attached to his keyring. 'You'll need that to slit my trousers.'

Kat threw him a regretful look. 'I hate the thought of ruining such beautiful tailoring,' she said, even as she began ripping them upwards from the hem.

'It'll be a lot less painful than trying to take them off,' he said with a groan as he dropped his head back on the jumper Josh had folded for him and left her to her task.

Once the trouser leg was stripped back to his knee, the injury was obvious—a textbook presentation. It was the work of seconds to check his capillary refill and that his reflexes were still working.

'Can you point your toes for me?' she asked, although there had been none of the 'six P's' signs of compartment syndrome evident, but if his attempt produced pain localised in his calf muscle then, whether he liked it or not, she was going to phone for an ambulance.

'No pain in the calf,' he confirmed with a significant glance in her direction that told her he had been concerned about the same complication. 'Initially, the leg was bent at a horrible angle. I think that by dragging myself out from under the car, I may have straightened it out and prevented circulatory complications.'

'But it's not a method I'd recommend,' she said sternly, as she padded the lengths of board Sam had found and placed wedges of towels between his ankles before Rose helped her to bind everything into position with several swift turns of bandage. The support he needed closer to the fracture was much more difficult, especially as she was all too aware that it would be the most painful.

Finally, she'd done as much as she was able and it was time to get him into the car.

'Sam, can you open the back door for us?' she directed, wondering how on earth she was going to get Ben up onto his feet, never mind getting him onto the back seat. He was definitely taller than her own five and a half feet—probably several inches over six—and while he looked as if he could do with carrying a bit more weight on his lean frame, it would still be more than enough as dead weight on her much slighter build.

She drew in a deep breath and approached his upper half, sitting him up being the first essential stage.

'If you can help me while I sit you up, well and good,' she said briskly to hide her trepidation. 'If it hurts too much, let me do all the work.'

His half-stifled groan told her that the manoeuvre *was* painful, but that didn't stop him doing more than his share of the work.

'Right. Catch your breath,' she suggested, while she tried to work out her next step to getting him vertical. She may as well have saved her breath.

Almost as soon as he was sitting upright he somehow managed to take the bulk of the weight of his torso onto his hands and drag himself along for nearly six inches.

'What do you think you're doing?' she demanded, too slow to prevent him doing it a second and a third time while she tried to work out how to stop him without hurting him.

'Positioning myself by the car door,' he said, his voice slightly laboured as the strenuous activity took its toll. 'There's no way someone your size could ever lift me, so we'll have to do it this way.'

Kat could see the logic of his decision, even as she deplored it. She only had his word and her own cursory examination to tell her that he hadn't sustained other injuries besides his broken leg. If there had been any spinal injuries...

She shuddered at the potential consequences.

'If only you'd let me call the ambulance,' she began, but

by that time he'd managed to position himself right against the side of her car with his back against the door opening.

'I'll need some help for this bit,' he admitted grimly, as though it went against the grain.

'You don't say,' she muttered under her breath as she stepped forward until her feet straddled his. 'What do you want me to do?'

'I'm going to have to do the next bit in two stages,' he explained, wiping a trickle of sweat from his forehead with an impatient swipe of one arm. 'Could you support my legs while I lift myself onto the sill and then again when I transfer up onto the seat?'

'Only if you promise that you'll tell me if I'm hurting you,' she insisted. 'I couldn't bear it if I were causing you more—'

'I'll be all right,' he broke in with a meaningful glance in her sons' direction, apparently more aware than she was that the two of them were hanging on every syllable of their conversation.

All she could do was send him a fierce glare that promised retribution at some later date.

'So, are you ready?' he said, and she knelt hurriedly to slide her arms around his legs, splints and all.

As if they'd practised the manoeuvre many times before, he put the heels of his hands on the sill behind him and with strength alone heaved himself off the ground. He was heavier than she'd expected, his thighs larger and far more muscular than she'd anticipated, but she managed to synchronise her effort exactly with his so that mere seconds later he had propped his hips on the sill between his hands.

'And again,' he directed, when he'd repositioned his hands to grip the door frame above his head, his voice definitely hoarser this time and his face so pale with the pain that it looked almost green. 'Now!'

And then he was sitting on the edge of the seat while she supported his legs and it was comparatively easy for him to shuffle backwards until his back was resting against the opposite door.

He leant his head back against the window but only allowed himself a couple of breaths to recover before he opened his eyes again.

'Can Josh come in the back with me?' he suggested. 'If he has something to pad his legs, could I rest mine on him?'

'Of course you can,' Josh declared almost eagerly. 'The hospital's not far…only about twenty minutes.'

Kat shut the door, leaving the two of them to settle Ben's weight to their satisfaction while she checked that Sam was safely belted in and hurried towards the driver's door.

'Do you want me to wait till you come back?' Rose asked, clearly flustered by such goings-on.

'No, Rose. You've done a full day,' Kat reminded her. 'If you could check with the on-call service to make sure that they're going to be picking up any after-hours calls and switch the phone through, that will be great. I'll see you in the morning.'

'Oh, please, Kat!' she exclaimed. 'You have to ring me when you get back from the hospital. I won't be able to sleep a wink until I know Dr Ben's going to be all right.'

'Only if I'm back before ten,' she conceded. 'You know how long it can take sometimes, waiting for X-rays and then finding out whether the leg can just be put in a cast or whether he'll need surgery.'

'The poor man!' Rose said softly, her pale blue eyes

showing her concern clearly. 'And all this because he worried more about saving Sam than himself.'

'What?' Kat wasn't certain what she meant. Sam had apologised for running behind the car, but…

'I thought you knew,' Rose said in surprise. 'I saw the whole thing out of the window. He saw what was going to happen and ran forward to push Sam out of the way. He just didn't have a chance to move far enough before the car hit him. Kat, he's a hero.'

CHAPTER TWO

HE'S a hero… The words played over and over in Ben's head as he waited interminably for his leg to be dealt with.

'Hah! If only they knew,' he muttered, startling the poor woman who'd been detailed to put the temporary backslab on his leg.

'I'm sorry. Did you say something?' she asked nervously with her plaster-coated hands suspended in mid-air. Perhaps it was the fact that he was a doctor, or perhaps it was nothing more than the scowl he could feel tugging at his face.

'No. *I'm* sorry,' he countered with a deliberately ingratiating smile. 'And I'm very grateful for the fact that you bumped me up to the head of the queue to get this job done.'

But in spite of that, he was very aware that Kat and her two sons were waiting for him out in the reception area. He'd tried to suggest that she should take Josh and Sam to their sports club, but both boys had protested vigorously, as had Kat when he'd proposed getting a taxi when he was released.

And he'd been determined he was going to be released, the sooner the better. Just spending this long in a hospital was stretching his nerves. If he never had to smell this dreadful mixture of antiseptic and death again, it would be too soon.

'Where will I have to go to get some crutches?' he asked, suddenly realising that no one had mentioned that important item of equipment.

'Oh, you don't have to worry about that today,' she said with a smile. 'The physiotherapy department will sort all that out. Your leg will be checked tomorrow morning to see whether we can put the fibreglass cast on and the physio will do the crutches thing before you're released. For now, you'll only need a wheelchair to get you up to the ward for a night on observation.'

Tension tightened round his head and his chest like steel bands.

'Except I'm not going up to the ward,' he pointed out through gritted teeth. 'My lift is waiting patiently to take me home, and she's a qualified doctor eminently qualified to do any necessary observations. So I'll need some crutches tonight.'

'Oh, but—'

'*Tonight*,' he repeated implacably, staring her earnest expression down and feeling like the worst kind of bully. 'With or without crutches.'

'I'll see what I can do,' she conceded as she bent to her task again, smoothing her hands over the wet plaster of the backslab.

Battle won, Ben idly watched the woman's experienced hands shaping and moulding the heavy material around his leg. He was contemplating just how lucky he'd been to sustain nothing more complicated than a clean fracture of his tibia when he found himself wondering whether it would feel any different if it were Kat applying the cast...having her slender, capable hands smoothing the finish from ankle to thigh, stroking the...

Whoa! Bad idea!

He didn't have those sorts of thoughts any more, especially while he was sitting in nothing more concealing than his underwear. Not since—He pulled his thoughts up short. That had been forbidden territory for the last three years. He didn't think about himself with a woman…*any* woman…any more, not even if the person in his imagination was slender and feminine with soft grey eyes and a sense of responsibility that was heavy enough to flatten a world-class weight-lifter.

'Right. That's it,' the nurse said briskly as she stepped over to the sink to rinse her hands and arms. 'Wait here for a minute while I see what I can do about some crutches. The backslab isn't hard, yet, so don't go moving your leg or you might crack it and displace the ends of the bone. And I'll need to get the doctor to sign you off,' she added at the last moment, almost running out of the plaster room, apparently keen to escape from his presence.

'Well, signature or not, I *will* be leaving,' he growled mutinously, only his fear of destroying all the woman's careful handiwork and having to have it done all over again preventing him from attempting to slide off the table straight away.

It was bad enough that he was going to have to come all the way back again tomorrow. Oh, he knew all the reasons why it was necessary. He'd seen the amount of swelling on his leg that, once it subsided, would leave any cast too ill-fitting to do its job.

It seemed for ever until she scurried back in with a pair of battered aluminium crutches clutched in one hand and a bundle of all-too-familiar green fabric in the other.

'I thought you might need something to put on,' she

offered, placing the scrubs on the table beside him. 'Your trousers are unlikely to fit over the slab.'

'My trousers are residing in a bin somewhere, cut to ribbons,' Ben said dryly. 'I'm very grateful you thought of this.' He shook them out and then realised that he had a major problem. His arms just weren't long enough to reach.

'Do you want me to call your wife in to give you a hand?' The nurse offered helpfully. 'She's going to be doing rather a lot of it over the next few weeks.'

'She's not my wife.' Pain made the words hard and abrupt but he only realised it when she took a step back and blinked. He forced himself to attempt a smile. 'Unfortunately, she's my new boss,' he confided, and threw her a wry grin as he gestured towards the backslab. 'This broken leg has probably lost me the job before I've even started it.'

It was strange, but that thought brought with it an unexpected feeling of disappointment.

'Well, the only way you'll find out is if you ask her, and you can't do that without some clothing on,' she pointed out, as she shook out the generously large scrubs trousers. 'Now, you'll find it easiest to put things on the broken leg first, as it's the least manoeuvrable.'

With the calm competence of an experienced nurse she was soon helping him to pull the gathered fabric up over his hips, and with a complete lack of fanfare put one shoe back on his foot. 'Hang on to the other one,' she instructed. 'You won't need it for a while, but you don't want it to get lost in the meantime.'

She bustled out of the room muttering, 'Now, where has that man got to…?' only to reappear just moments later with a burly porter in tow with a wheelchair.

'I don't need that. You brought me some crutches,' he protested, hating the idea of being dependent on anybody.

'Trust me when I tell you that you'll need this, at least until you get proficient with the crutches,' she warned. 'And the leg extension attachment will help to protect the slab while it's still hardening. It'll take several hours when the plaster's this thick.'

He subsided with bad grace, uncomfortably aware that he was behaving every bit as impatiently as Kat's boys had, but *they* were only kids. He was a rational adult male who ought to be able to mind his manners better.

The transfer from table to wheelchair was awkward and ungainly and he hated the lack of control he had over his own body, but eventually he was safely settled in the despised thing.

He gave a huge sigh. None of his problems were her fault and yet he'd been taking his frustrations out on the poor woman. 'I'm sorry I've been such a grouch,' he said, looking up at her penitently.

'Don't worry about it,' she said, her tone almost patronising. For one awful moment he almost thought that she was going to pat him on his head. 'You're a doctor. We expect it of you when you're the patient.'

'Hmm! Watch it, or I'll take my apology back,' he threatened.

'Can't be done. Not until you can run faster than I can,' she said with a smug little wave of her hand as he was wheeled out of the door, clutching the plastic bag that contained the contents of his trouser pockets, a bottle of painkillers, a pair of crutches and a single shoe.

Still, she was good at her job, he mused, remembering her

swift expertise. He could do far worse than find her on duty when he returned tomorrow for the fibreglass version.

'There he is, Mum,' called a childish voice. 'There's Dr Ben…and he's got an enormous cast on! It's *humungous!*'

And there they were, waiting for him, Sam wide-eyed and once again bouncing around, Josh trying hard to seem worldly-wise but still visibly impressed by the bulky green-clad burden stuck out for all the world to see. And Kat…sweet Kat, whose fragility and vulnerability he shouldn't even be noticing, was standing with her keys clenched tightly in her hand, her soft grey eyes examining him carefully as he was wheeled towards her little family.

'They said you insisted on coming out tonight.' Concern was clear as she examined his ungainly leg and the bottle of painkillers. He doubted he looked like anyone's idea of an ideal house guest.

'I hate hospitals,' he growled, startling a giggle out of Sam. 'But don't tell anyone,' he added conspiratorially. 'If doctors say that, they get a black mark.'

'Well, we'd better get you out of here before anyone over-hears you,' Kat suggested with a tired smile that piled several layers of guilt on top of the mountain he already carried. The poor woman already had enough responsibilities on her plate. She certainly didn't need him adding to them.

And yet…somehow he couldn't make himself say the words that would set her free to go on her way. Something inside him was telling him that it was important that he should go home with her little family, that it would be a good thing, but whether that was going to be a good thing for him or for them, he couldn't guess.

'Are you going to be all right in the back with me, Josh? My leg's even heavier this time,' he warned.

'Yeah, but it's only *one* leg, so that should make it the same as the two together when we were coming to the hospital,' he pointed out with perfect childish logic. 'Can I push you to the car?'

'No! I want to push him,' objected Sam. 'You're going to have his leg on you all the way home so it won't be fair if you're the one who pushes him, too!'

'I think we're all going to have to take turns pushing,' Kat mediated swiftly, before the argument could escalate. 'Remember how far away I had to park the car?'

'How about if you go to get the car and drive it right up to the entrance?' Ben suggested, hating the thought that a woman who was already tired to the bone would have to exhaust herself still further. 'You could leave Josh and Sam with me…to take care of me,' he added quickly, in case boyish sensibilities were bruised.

He watched those soft grey eyes take in each of her sons' responses to the suggestion before replying.

'If you don't mind waiting while I get it. It shouldn't take me more than a couple of minutes.'

'Don't hurry,' he said with a sudden flash of inspiration. 'It they're as hungry as I am, the boys and I will be discussing the relative merits of the various take-away establishments between the hospital and home.' And when she looked as if she was going to argue against the idea, he added, 'I just don't feel up to cooking for myself tonight, and the boys would be very late to bed if they have to wait for you to make something once you get home.'

'That seems sensible,' she agreed blandly, but he caught

a glimpse of a keen intelligence behind those soft grey eyes that warned him she wouldn't allow him to manipulate her into doing anything she didn't really want to, no matter how much easier it might make her life.

And she certainly needed her life made easier, he realised when he and the two boys tucked into steaming plates of pizza at the kitchen table while she barely sat down.

In the time that it took him to fill the gnawing hollow inside, she'd put a load of washing in the machine, prepared lunch boxes for Josh and Sam for the next day and put them in the fridge ready for the morning and had made several forays out of the room that involved strange unidentified thumps that were only explained when she sent the boys off to the bathroom to get ready for bed.

'While you've got that temporary cast on you won't be able to get up the stairs, so I've put you in one of the rooms down on this level…if that's all right with you. I thought it would be safer while you're getting used to using the crutches.'

His first instinct was to object. The very idea of sharing a relatively small space with Kat and her two sons would be too much to cope with, especially if she'd given up her own room for him.

While he'd been trying to find the words to turn down the offer, she'd quietly taken charge of the wheelchair and without any fuss had piloted him along the hall.

'There are the stairs,' she said, pointing to the wrought-iron spiral of steps rising from the corner of the hallway through a circular hole in the ceiling—obviously impossible for a leg in a cast, as she had known. 'And here is the bedroom with a bathroom opening directly off it.'

Kat pushed him into a room that was much bigger than he'd expected, but every breath he took told him that this was her private space he was invading.

There was nothing overtly fussy or flowery about the décor, everything in shades of calm neutrals with accents of a soft sage green. But it smelt like she did, of something not quite flowery but not spicy either. Whatever it was, it wasn't helping that he was looking at the freshly made bed that she'd been sleeping in last night. And that was another thing he shouldn't be thinking about.

'The previous GP who lived here put in this bathroom when his wife had a stroke,' she said as she pushed him to the open door, continuing with her low-key guided tour. 'As you can see, it's got a walk-in shower with a seat that folds away. I thought that would be much easier to cope with unaided if you taped some plastic around the top of your leg to protect your cast.'

He sighed silently, conceding that she was right. He was in no fit state to clamber up those stairs and a bath would be beyond him.

'I don't like putting you out of your room,' he pointed out uncomfortably, wondering if he would be able to sleep, knowing it was her bed. 'I'll stay in here just for a few days…until I get proficient on the crutches.'

'Take your time,' she said. 'It's no problem for me to use the other room.' She left him for a moment and returned with the small stash of belongings he'd carried home from the hospital, depositing the plastic bag on the bedside cabinet and propping the crutches against the bed. Her second journey had her returning with the suitcase he'd stowed in the back of his car, last seen parked in front of the practice.

'You didn't have to do that,' he objected, his protective male instincts rebelling against the thought of someone as slight as Kat hefting such a heavy weight. She threw a wry glance in the direction of his bulky leg, pointing out without saying a word that *he* certainly wasn't in a fit state to carry anything, and he subsided glumly.

'It hardly seems worthwhile bringing everything in when I won't be staying long,' he said, when she returned with the last of his luggage. 'You'll be needing the room for whoever takes the job.'

'But the job's yours!' she exclaimed, clearly startled. 'It's my fault that you've been injured, so it's my responsibility to look after you until you're on your feet again.'

That was just what he didn't want…to be another responsibility for her to carry on those slender shoulders. But the alternative—to leave Ditchling without ever having a chance to get to know this courageous woman—was unthinkable, too.

'I can't just be a burden on you,' he objected. 'The whole reason why you were advertising for an associate was because you're either rushed off your feet without a minute to call your own, or you're paying vast sums for other people to cover for you.'

'Mum! Can you come and hear me read?' called Sam, his voice loud in the sudden silence between them.

'Coming!' she called back. 'Have you brushed your teeth?'

She paused in the doorway, almost as if she was momentarily suspended between her roles of mother and GP. 'We'll talk about this when I've finished settling the boys down. There must be something…'

That little pleat was back between those silky eyebrows and he was struck by the sudden urge to smooth it away with a fingertip…or a kiss.

'Enough!' he growled to himself as soon as she was out of earshot. 'You don't need any complications in your life, especially ones that come with children, no matter how tempting their mother is.

'And she doesn't even realise just how…' He was lost for words, searching for them inside a head that could only think about how much the light fragrance surrounding him suited her.

'Is this some sort of reaction to the accident? Did they give me something in A and E that's scrambled my brain?'

The only solution was, as ever, hard work that left him no time to think.

'Time to unpack,' he decided, gripping the wheel-rims of the chair and turning it laboriously around.

It didn't take him long to discover that making the decision wasn't the same as carrying it out. Even the smaller of his two suitcases was beyond him when he couldn't use his lower body to help him lift it onto the bed, and that would be the only level at which he could reach into it.

He paused for a moment, slumped in the hated chair and muttering swearwords under his breath when he had the prickling sensation that someone was watching him.

A quick glance over his shoulder told him the worst and a wave of guilt swept over him that he'd been caught setting such a bad example.

'Sorry about the bad language,' he said flatly. There was a brief flash of surprise on the youngster's face, as though he hadn't expected an apology from him, but he could tell that their brief truce surrounding his injury was over.

Josh's hackles were up again.

'This was my dad's room…and my mum's,' he announced truculently, letting Ben know in no uncertain terms that his presence wasn't welcome on such hallowed ground. But Josh hadn't finished. 'My mum's a widow but she still loves my dad,' he added fiercely, and Ben wondered just how badly his usual control had slipped. Had his unexpected response to Kat been so obvious that even an eleven-year-old had noticed? It was time for some judicious damage control.

'Good,' he said with an approving nod. 'That's how it *should* be in a good marriage.' *Hah!* The little voice inside his head commented. *What would you know about it? You couldn't even…*

'So, why has Mum put you in here?' Josh demanded, childish frustration at the incomprehensibility of adult actions spilling over. 'It's *her* room now. And you're supposed to be upstairs in the flat.'

'And I would be if it weren't for *this*.' Ben knocked his knuckles on the cast draped in voluminous pale green cotton. 'I can't manage stairs with it yet, but in a couple of days…' He shrugged, hoping it looked nonchalant enough to convince Josh's protective instincts. Once more he reached for the suitcase and this time tried to swing it up onto the bed. Instead, he nearly toppled the wheelchair over and wrenched some of the more tender areas of his back.

He only just managed to hold in a curse but thought the effort well worthwhile when he caught a glimpse of sympathy replacing the animosity in Josh's stance.

'I could help you with that,' he suggested suddenly, and Ben blinked in surprise. Unfortunately he was going to have to refuse.

'I think it would be too heavy for you to lift. I'm afraid I usually pack too many books,' he added hurriedly when Josh began to look affronted, obviously seeing his refusal as a slight.

'Could we do it together?' Josh offered, for the first time moving further into the room than his defensive position in the doorway.

Agreement was Ben's only option. For Kat's sake he had to get on with her sons if he could. He was already a major burden on her. A bad atmosphere in the house might be the final straw.

'We could give it a go,' Ben agreed, as he wheeled the chair back a little to allow him to take up position on the other side of the case. 'How do you suggest we go about it?'

It was the work of mere seconds after that to decide on a likely method and to implement it.

'That was completely painless,' Ben said, as he reached forward to unzip the case and flip the lid back.

To his surprise, Josh burst into chuckles.

Ben couldn't help an answering grin when he saw just how untidy it looked.

'That's what *my* suitcase looked like when I tried to pack it,' Josh confided. 'I had to get Mum to do it for me because I couldn't fit everything in.'

'Perhaps it's a woman thing…being able to pack a case properly?' Ben suggested, and had to stifle another smile when he saw Josh considering the idea so seriously.

'Probably,' Josh pronounced several seconds later with a decisive nod. 'And they like everything else to be tidy, too, so you have to put your laundry in the basket and make your bed and put your toys away.' He sighed heavily.

'I can remember *my* mother making me do all that,' Ben agreed, only too willing to foster the glimmer of a bond. He lifted his wash bag out of the suitcase, deposited it on his lap and started turning the wheelchair to take it to the bathroom.

'I could take that through for you,' Josh suggested diffidently. 'I'll put it beside the basin.'

Ben caught his eye and when he saw the answering gleam of mirth they added in unison, 'Tidily!'

An hour later, Ben collapsed into bed completely exhausted. He would never have believed how much energy it took just to get himself undressed and washed. It had probably been a wise decision not to practise getting about on the crutches tonight. He'd probably have fallen flat on his face and broken something else.

The trouble was, even though he was physically tired, his brain was still wide awake, contemplating the consequences of his temporary disability.

Obviously, I won't be able to drive anywhere for a while, he thought dryly, trying to imagine how far back he would have to push the seat to get the cast into the car. Would he even be able to reach the steering-wheel?

But if he wasn't going to be able to do the home visits that Kat wanted her associate to take over for her, then, in all conscience, he should go so that she could find someone else who could.

Except...

Except he didn't want to go, he admitted reluctantly and sighed.

For three years he'd had an absolute rule of non-involvement, but within hours of meeting Kat and her little family— and in spite of ending up with a broken leg—there was something about all three of them that made him reluctant to leave Kat to struggle on alone. So, he had a major problem. He didn't want to leave, at least until she'd found someone suitable to take his place, but in his present state he was worse than useless. If only there was some way he could…

Kat had come to a decision while she'd been finishing off the evening's list in the never-ending round of chores.

It didn't matter that he couldn't do anything to help her at the practice, it was her responsibility to take care of Ben until he was well enough to travel back to his home. And it was time she reassured him of that fact. After all, if she were in the same position, she would want to know exactly where she stood…or *sat* in his case, she tacked on with a wry smile.

'Ben…' she called softly, tapping on the door to what had been her sanctuary since Richard's death.

'Come in,' the husky voice invited, but when she opened the door and saw him propped up in her bed, naked to the waist, she almost dropped the steaming mug in her other hand.

'I…I'm sorry. I wouldn't have disturbed you if I'd known that you were… I only wanted to…' For heaven's sake! What was the matter with her? She'd seen a semi-naked man in that bed every night of her married life.

But never one with such a broad muscular chest, decorated with a thick swathe of dark silky-looking hair from one dusky nipple to the other, countered that dratted voice in her head.

'I heard you telling the boys that you still enjoyed a mug of hot chocolate,' she said, hastily diverting her eyes from the stunning view in front of her to the prosaic white mug. 'And I thought I ought to have a word with you…'

'Come in and shut the door,' he invited, and he must have seen her surprise at the unexpected request because he quickly added, 'So that we don't disturb Sam and Josh.'

Kat felt a swift rush of heat scorching her cheeks. As if she had to worry about her reputation with a man like him. If he was looking for a relationship, he certainly wouldn't be interested in a permanently exhausted mother of two.

'I was thinking…about you and the job,' she began tentatively. 'Of course, you're welcome to stay here until you're fit enough to go home, but—'

'Kat, before you say any more, can I ask you a favour?' he interrupted, just when she was getting into her stride. 'You see, I haven't got a home to go to at the moment.'

'What?' she exclaimed, unable to believe such an outlandish statement.

'It's true,' he said with a tired smile. 'It had been on the market for ages and suddenly I had a purchaser who was in a hurry to buy. So, rather than lose the sale, I packed everything up and moved it into storage just a couple of days ago, then was told about the vacancy here.' He caught her eyes with his, their clear green almost seeming to envelop her in the calming hush of a leafy sunlit glade before he continued, 'If you kick me out, I'll have nowhere to go…at least, nowhere so suitable for life in a wheelchair or on crutches.'

'But…the job,' Kat said helplessly, even as a minor war was being fought inside her. She had a niggling feeling that she was being manipulated in some way but that was completely vanquished by the impossible elation caused by the fact that he might *not* be leaving after all.

'Yes. The job.' He paused for a moment in thought, looking up at her from under those thick dark lashes. 'I've been thinking about that, and I wondered… Well, I know it's going to take me a few days before I'm really competent on the crutches, but once I am, I should easily be able to get from here to the practice. And if you're happy to do the leg-work…the home visits and so on…I would still be pulling my weight.'

How could she refuse? she asked herself even as she admitted that she really didn't *want* to refuse. To put it bluntly, she needed his help. And it was all very well ratio-nalising that it was her duty to accommodate him because it was her fault that he'd been injured, but the plain fact of the matter was that there was something about the man that called to her…that made her feel things that she'd believed were gone for ever.

'It's pointless thinking about him that way,' she whispered into the darkness, once she'd silently made her way up the spiral staircase and slipped into the bed that should have been his. 'He's a drifter, so he's the last person I could ever get involved with, no matter if he does set my hormones buzzing.'

The boys wouldn't understand, and would be hurt if she had a relationship with the man, only to have him leave at the end of his contract. They'd been devastated when Richard had died. Heaven only knew what sort of psychological damage it would do to them if they grew close to another man, only to have him leave.

CHAPTER THREE

'How soon will it be before Dr Leeman finishes surgery?' enquired a male voice, just as Ben was preparing to leave the room Kat had allocated to him.

'Oh, hello, Mr Sadowski,' Rose said cheerfully. 'Did you want an appointment?'

'Not this time,' he said, and something about his tone of voice set every one of the hairs up on the back of Ben's neck.

Depositing the pile of patient notes in their tray, ready for Rose to collect, he reached for his crutches.

He arrived in the reception area just as Rose put the call through to Kat's room.

'Dr Leeman, there's a gentleman here to see you,' she said formally. 'It's Mr Sadowski, from the chemist,' she added. She waited a moment for Kat to speak then said, 'I'll tell him,' and put the phone down. 'She'll be out in a minute,' she told the newcomer. 'If you'd like to take a seat while you're waiting?'

Ben took the last few hobbling steps to the counter, envying the other man the easy way he sauntered across the room. It felt like years since he'd been able to do that when, in fact, it had only been a little over a week. At least most of that time had been spent in a modern lightweight fibreglass cast rather than the heavy temporary plaster of Paris one.

'I've left the files on the desk, Rose,' he murmured to the bustling receptionist. 'I'm sorry it's giving you extra work to fetch them, but I just can't manage to carry the basket through with these wretched things.' He waved a battered crutch.

'Don't you worry about that, Dr Ben,' Rose said with a fond smile, using the more formal form of address in front of the other man. When it was only the practice staff on the premises, they all went by first names. 'You've taken such a load off Dr Leeman just by being here that I'd gladly fetch and carry all day.'

'Hmm! Perhaps you shouldn't have told me that,' he teased, liking the down-to-earth little woman more and more the longer he knew her, not least for the way she clucked over Kat and her boys. 'I might be tempted to take advantage of you.'

It sounded almost as if the man waiting impatiently by the pile of magazines and children's books muttered something like, 'As if you aren't already,' but the words were half-buried under Rose's laughter.

And then Kat came out with her own basket of patient notes and when Ben saw the avid expression on the other man's face he suddenly understood only too well what was going on.

'Mr Sadowski?' she said politely when she recognised him, and the sharp claws of jealousy loosened their grip a little.

'Greg,' he said with a smile, but Ben could see from the tension around the man's eyes that he was not happy to be having this meeting in front of so many witnesses.

He had no intention of leaving.

'Ah, Rose said you weren't here for an appointment?' The raised tone at the end of the sentence made it into a question.

'No. Um, actually, I was here to, um, well…to ask if you'd thought any more about that invitation?'

'Invitation?' Her forehead pleated in puzzlement and Ben nearly chuckled aloud. Kat really had no idea what the man had in mind, which meant that there was almost no chance that she was attracted to him. Although why that should matter to *him* was something he would have to think about later.

For now, he was enjoying watching the man sweat a little while he tried to make-believe he was a smooth man of the world, when in actual fact he obviously came nowhere near deserving a woman like Kat.

'Um, the dinner-dance? This Saturday?'

This was almost painful, but Ben didn't want to miss a delicious moment of it, especially as Kat was apparently oblivious to the fact the man was almost hyperventilating, waiting for her answer.

'Oh, Mr…Greg, I'm sorry, but I couldn't possibly. I'm on call all this weekend.' And the sooner Ben was able to take that chore from her, the better, he thought darkly, hating the idea that he wasn't pulling his weight on such an exhausting part of the workload.

Ben saw the man throw a glare in his direction and, guessing what was coming, leant back against the reception counter and deliberately crossed his broken leg in front of the good one.

'Oh, but surely that's why you employed…' Too late he realised his mistake.

'Sorry, old man, but I can't even get behind the wheel at the moment, let alone drive out to do a house call,' Ben said smugly, knowing he was putting an end to the man's dreams. 'And, anyway, if I was called out, who would look after Josh and Sam if Kat was out with you? I certainly couldn't take them with me and they're too young to be left alone.'

'But…' Ben had to give him his due—the man didn't want to admit defeat—but this time it was Kat who interrupted.

'I'm sorry…Greg. It was good of you to think of me but, as you can see, my life is a bit complicated at the moment. Perhaps another time…?'

It was beautifully done, with regret for turning him down sweetened with the possibility of another chance at some unspecified time in the future, but Greg definitely wasn't happy about it. Man to man, he probably *knew* that Ben would be gloating over seeing him turned down because *he* would have in the same situation.

'Dr Leeman?' Rose interrupted the charged silence. 'You haven't forgotten that the boys need collecting from sports club tonight?'

'Tonight?' Kat whirled to face Rose and Ben nearly chortled aloud at the faces Rose was pulling to stop Kat pointing out that it had been sports club night yesterday. 'Ah, yes. Thank you for reminding me, Rose. I'd better go and get my keys now, or I'll be late.' She turned back to the chemist briefly. 'I'm sorry to have to dash off, but thank you for your invitation,' she said like a well brought-up child then walked briskly out of the room.

'Well, that's my cue to get the meal on the table,' Ben said casually, as he adjusted his grip on the crutches and straightened up to his full height, stupidly pleased to note that he topped the other man by nearly half a head. 'The boys like it to be ready when they get home so they have time to do their homework before bedtime.' And if that didn't sound cosily domestic, nothing did, he thought as he turned his back on the man, only to catch Rose trying to wipe a grin from her face.

'And it's time I finished putting these files away and locked up,' she volunteered briskly, picking up the basket Kat had brought through. 'Tomorrow will be here soon enough. Goodnight, Dr Ben. Say goodnight to Dr Leeman for me, will you?'

'Oh, I will, Rose. I will,' Ben called over his shoulder, as he left the building and made his way as swiftly as he could safely manage round the corner of the practice in case the disappointed suitor should see him laughing.

'Rose, could you ask Mrs Couling to come through, please?'

Kat paused just long enough for the receptionist's murmured reply before putting the receiver down, then blew out a steady stream of air through pursed lips and marvelled that the embarrassment was still there, just as fiercely, several days later.

She'd never been a social butterfly, even as a teenager. She'd been far too focused on her goal of becoming a doctor for anything but the most cursory of dates until she'd met Richard part way through her training.

'I just hadn't realised how clueless I was,' she muttered, and the heat surged into her cheeks all over again when she remembered looking out of the window to see when her unexpected visitor left, and had caught sight of Ben laughing himself silly.

That had been when the penny had dropped.

Until that moment, she honestly hadn't realised that the

pharmacist had any sort of intentions towards her. Perhaps the fact that it had now been more than a year since Richard had died should have reminded her of the strange conversation she'd had with him some weeks ago. À *propos* of absolutely nothing, he'd started talking about the fact that he was a very traditional sort of man who liked the 'old ways'. Looking back on it, had that been his way of telling her that he waiting until the old-fashioned 'year of mourning' was over before he felt free to ask her out?

Ben had certainly understood what had been going on and had been highly amused, but had it been necessary for him to laugh like that? At least he'd spared Mr…something…George? No, *Greg*…Greg Sadowski. At least he'd been spared the humiliation of knowing that he was the butt of the joke.

The tap at the door was almost a relief.

'Come in, Mrs Couling,' she said with a smile. 'How can I help you?

'Well, I've been having some problems with my eyes, but when I went to my optician for my regular check-up, he said it was cataracts but it wasn't anything to worry about yet. That it was too soon to have surgery.'

'But you're still worried?' That fact was obvious to Kat.

'I'm a widow and I'm eighty-one and my car is the only means I have of getting around. My eyes are already bad enough that I'm only able to distinguish writing on a page with one eye and I'm worried that, if the optician delays getting my name on the operating list, I'll end up unable to drive.'

Kat understood only too well how widowhood could leave a person feeling isolated. At least she had her health and strength and her two beautiful boys. Not that Ruth Couling was weak and feeble. Just a few moments of conversation had told Kat that her mind was still as sharp as a tack and she had numerous grandchildren she would miss out on seeing…literally…if she couldn't drive any more.

'So, you'd like me to refer you to someone to give you a second opinion—preferably the surgeon who would be doing the job?' Kat suggested.

'Well, I can't honestly see any point in delaying,' the spry little woman said sensibly. 'I'm already eighty-one. They tell me these replacement lenses will last for years, so why can't I have them now, when I'll be able to make the most use of them?'

The strange thing was, Kat thought, returning to her previous train of thought, Ben's amusement at her expense didn't seem to have made any difference to the way he treated her, either in the practice or after work. And they were certainly seeing far more of each other than she'd expected when she'd offered him accommodation.

Changing his cast for the fibreglass one hadn't happened until later, but as soon as he'd gained any sort of proficiency on those disreputable crutches, Ben had insisted on starting work.

It was as if the local population had been holding back in deference to her single practitioner status, because almost from the day he'd sat behind Richard's desk, the number of patients wanting an appointment had nearly doubled.

'I don't know where they're all coming from, I'm sure,' Rose had commented in exasperation when she had to check with Kat whether she had time to squeeze another couple in that afternoon. 'Having Ben here was supposed to make your life easier.'

'But it has, Rose,' Kat defended rather too fast to be seemly. 'Since he's been here, I haven't had to pay an extortionate amount for someone to cover the call-outs at night, and the fact that he's here, in the house, means I haven't had to worry about the boys either.'

'They've certainly taken to him,' Rose said with a smile, then raised a significant eyebrow. 'You could do a lot worse, you know.'

'Rose!' Kat felt herself blushing at the thought of what her receptionist was suggesting. 'You know very well that he's only here for a while. In fact, as today is the last day of his "on trial" fortnight, he could tell me he's not happy with things and he'd be gone before the weekend.'

'Or he could stay for the full six months and decide he doesn't want to leave at all,' Rose pointed out earnestly. 'He's certainly got a pair of sharp eyes in his head and most of the time they're looking in your direction.'

Probably waiting for the next demonstration of her social ineptitude, she thought uncharitably.

'You know as well as I do how unlikely that is,' Kat chided. 'He's a drifter, and the boys need something more than that.'

'Doesn't mean that he can't help them in the meantime,' Rose said staunchly. 'I know Josh will be a hard nut to crack. He was old enough to understand more of what his daddy was going through, and he's put up a wall to protect himself. Sam…' She smiled. 'You can already see the difference in Sam.'

She was right.

In just two weeks of Ben's presence, Sam had almost reverted to his old happy-go-lucky self. Often now she heard his infectious giggle pealing through the air as Ben tried to coach him in the finer points of football…on crutches.

As for Josh…Rose was right about the way he'd withdrawn after Richard's death. He had been like a plant loath to put out new shoots after a bad frost, and until he got that courage back, he wouldn't be able to grow properly.

Still, his school work had improved by leaps and bounds with Ben's undivided attention. She wasn't quite sure how it had happened. Perhaps it had started with a one-off question in the half-hour after Sam had gone to bed, but now Ben was just as likely to spend that time going over Josh's homework with him or helping him with a topic that didn't quite make sense as spending it completing some of the never-ending paperwork or watching television.

Sometimes he even stayed downstairs to watch a programme with her, as though he couldn't be bothered to make the effort to struggle up those spiral stairs until the last possible moment.

Not that he was content with the situation as it was, she admitted to herself in the brief pause between patients, knowing she'd have a minute or two before Mr Aldarini reached her surgery. Without him having to say a single word, Ben's dissatisfaction was clear every time the phone rang and Kat had to drive to an out-of-hours patient.

'Half of these journeys are totally unnecessary,' he'd growled when she'd returned from a visit to a patient 'in agony with appendicitis' who'd only needed a laxative, only to be called out straight away by someone who hadn't had time to ask for a repeat prescription for painkillers and had now run out.

'So they may be,' she'd said then had given a resigned shrug.

'But you know as well as I do that we have to go, just in case it really had been appendicitis, or even something worse.'

'We'd never forgive ourselves,' he'd conceded. 'But it's just because of our dedication that the time-wasters know they can get away with it. Sometimes it makes me wish we could charge them, because one day the wasted call-out will prevent us getting to a genuine patient and there could be disastrous consequences.'

'Sorry to take so long,' said Mr Aldarini as he subsided gratefully into the chair on the other side of the desk, his musical Italian accent still as strong as the day he'd left his native country.

'So, what can I do for you today?' Kat asked, sidestepping his apology. She'd been trying to persuade him that it was time for a hip replacement for nearly a year now, but his morbid fear of hospitals had overridden her advice every time.

'Please, *dottoressa,* you can make me an appointment to see the man at the hospital,' he announced with a resigned air. 'I know I will probably die in that terrible place, but the pain…' He shook his head. 'The pain will kill me if the hospital doesn't, so I must take my chances.'

For a moment Kat couldn't believe what she was hearing. She'd been convinced that the stubborn old man was going to resist to the end. The only trouble now was that he would have months to wait before it was his turn for surgery. Unless…

She reached for the phone. 'Rose, could you get me the number of that new orthopaedic surgeon…the recent appointment? There was an article in the local paper…' She searched her brain for the name but it was elusive.

'Mr Khan,' Rose supplied. 'Hang on a moment and I'll get it straight away.'

It was less than a minute later when she rang back. 'Dr Leeman, I have Mr Khan's secretary on the phone for you.' Kat stifled a smile. Did Rose's amazing speed mean that she had the same fear that Mr Aldarini might change his mind unless they got everything booked as soon as possible?

'Hello, I'm Kat Leeman out at Ditchling and I have a gentleman here in a pretty bad way,' she announced briskly. 'He badly needs an urgent hip replacement but until now he's been adamant about not going into hospital.'

'I take it he's just changed his mind.' The voice on the other end sounded wry. It probably wasn't the first time she'd heard that story, especially when the news was so full of stories about hospital-acquired infections and unnecessary deaths.

'The thing is, I was wondering if there was any way we could fast-track him?' Kat asked. 'I could arrange from this end to have the necessary X-rays done, but I was thinking…would it be possible to put his name down for the first short-notice cancellation?'

'You mean, when someone's been called in and for some reason their operation can't be performed?'

'Exactly!' Kat was cheered by the woman's friendly reception. 'We're about a twenty-minute drive away so—'

'Hang on a minute,' she interrupted hastily, and put her hand over the mouthpiece. Kat subsided, able to decipher enough of the muffled noises to hear the woman explaining her request to someone in the room with her.

'Dr Leeman?' She was back again. 'Mr Khan says it's always helpful to have someone willing to fill a slot at short notice. He says will you send the patient in tomorrow morning with a letter of referral? He may have a little time to wait as Mr Khan will be fitting him in between the other patients, but he should then be able to send him to have the necessary X-rays taken before he goes home again. After that, it would be a matter of waiting for the phone to ring. Would that be acceptable to your patient?'

Kat relayed the message to the man in the seat opposite her, wondering if her expression was as full of amazement as her patient's. She certainly hadn't expected to get a response this quickly.

'You are sure this is a real surgeon?' he demanded warily. 'My neighbour, he had to wait for months for even the first appointment. It was nearly a year before the operation came.'

'Yes, Mr Aldarini, I am certain he's a real surgeon,' Kat said with a laugh. 'He's a new one, so perhaps he has more space on his list than your friend's surgeon. So, do you want me to tell him you will be there tomorrow morning?'

'*Si, dottoressa,*' he said, but the excitement that things were moving so quickly was mixed with fear. 'I will go, but I will ask many questions about infections in the hospital and how many of this man's patients are dying.'

'I heard that, loud and clear,' chuckled the secretary on the other end of the line. 'It sounds as if he's going to make sure we're on our toes.'

'I wouldn't doubt it for a minute,' Kat agreed. 'Now, how much information do you need today, or can I send everything in with Mr Aldarini tomorrow morning?'

'There!' Kat exclaimed when she sat back a couple of minutes later. 'Everything is arranged except your transport. Will you need to order a taxi or—'

'That is no problem,' the elderly man said dismissively, the problem of transport just a minor concern against the excitement of getting an appointment so quickly. 'My neighbour has said he will drive me whenever the appointment comes… You know, *his* hip was so bad that before his operation he couldn't drive at all. Now he is here…there…out visiting friends…' The expressive hand gestures were telling the story all by themselves. 'He says that when it is my appointment he can visit the pretty nurses who took care of him.'

He was still thanking her effusively as he left her room, but Kat was crossing her fingers. Mr Aldarini's hips had been in a bad way when she'd first suggested he needed replacement surgery. His fear and stubbornness meant that a lot of time had passed while the disease process had continued to worsen. She was hoping that the surgeon wouldn't discover that there was some reason why the operation couldn't now be done.

'That last patient of yours certainly sounded as if he thought you could walk on water,' Ben commented teasingly as they met in the short corridor, and Kat's silly heart leapt in spite of all her best intentions.

'It's nothing,' she began dismissively, then changed her mind and decided to see if she could surprise him. 'Mr Aldarini has been resisting the idea of going into hospital to have hip replacement surgery. Finally, the pain got so bad that he decided to brave his fears. He came in today to ask me to refer him to an orthopaedic surgeon.'

'I don't understand.' He frowned. 'You can't have explained how long he's going to have to wait to see anyone, or he wouldn't be looking so cheerful.'

'On the contrary, he's looking so cheerful *because* he

knows when he's going to see the surgeon.' She paused deliberately before serving the ace. 'The appointment's tomorrow morning.'

'What?' *There* was the disbelief she'd been looking for. It was like balm to her soul and went a long way to soothing the ego bruised by his laughter. 'That's impossible!'

'Not if you know the right people.' She preened, breathing on her nails and buffing them on her suit jacket.

'Tell me!' he demanded, following close behind her as she led the way into Reception. 'What's the secret?'

'A secret? Who's got a secret?' demanded Rose avidly, her eyes flicking from one to the other. 'Or is it something… personal?'

For several heartbeats the idea of something personal and secret between the two of them filled the scant inches separating Ben's shoulder from Kat's and Kat could have sworn she heard the crackle of electricity.

'Nothing *that* exciting, Rose,' Ben said, and Kat was glad that one of them had managed to find their tongue and sound so offhand. She was still trying to subdue the pictures forming inside her head to stop herself blushing. 'I was only trying to persuade Kat to tell me her secret for getting orthopaedic patients appointments at such short notice, but she wasn't saying. Do you think I should try bribing her?'

'Or you could try bribing me instead,' Rose offered cheekily, the eyes sparkling up at him from behind her glasses like those of a woman a decade younger. 'I'm open to all offers of chocolates. A nice big box of really dark ones and I'll tell you whatever you want to know.'

'Rose! You're bribable! A woman after my own heart,' he exclaimed, and held out a crooked elbow as his hands were both fully occupied with his crutches. 'Come through to my office and let's see if we can strike a deal.'

'Don't you dare, Rose,' Kat admonished teasingly, joining in with their silly five minutes. 'I'll give you *two* boxes if you maintain your silence.'

'Ah. The boss lady's playing tough,' Ben said musingly, narrowing those gleaming green eyes so that he was peering from one to the other through those ridiculously long lashes. 'So, what if I were to throw in a bottle of champagne?'

'And I offered two,' Kat trumped him immediately, amazed to realise just how much fun this was.

'And a slap-up meal at a restaurant of your choice,' he suggested with the despairing air of a man who knows he's not going to win.

'For two,' Kat added.

'Hmm!' Rose mused, tapping a fingertip to her pursed lips. 'I've got a better idea, Ben. Give the chocolates and champagne to Kat and take *her* out for the meal and she'll probably tell you herself.'

'Rose!' Kat gasped, almost speechless with the speed that the tables had been turned on them. She was also uncomfortably aware that the idea of sharing a special meal with Ben was more attractive than it should be, especially when she knew just how little respect he had for her social charms. It would be a long time before she forgot the way he'd laughed…

'So, what do you say, boss lady?' Ben wheedled, turning those mesmerising eyes full on her and sending a shiver of awareness right through her. 'If I ply you with goodies, will you tell me your secret?'

'I couldn't possibly…go out for a meal with you,' she stumbled, and the unexpected flash of hurt in his eyes made her realise that she'd put her refusal badly. 'We can't go out together… The practice…I'm on call and you're home, keeping an ear open for the boys.'

'Well, *that's* easily solved,' Rose interrupted far too swiftly, and Kat got a sinking feeling in her stomach. 'You can use the on-call service for a night without breaking the bank, Kat, and I'm very happy to sit with Josh and Sam. I can use them for practice for when the grandchildren come. Anyway, you've got better television reception than I have *and* more channels.' She barely paused to draw breath as she turned back to her ominously silent companion. 'So, Ben, have you decided which restaurant you're taking her to?'

'Oh, but you can't…I mean… Just because Rose…' She trailed off to a halt when she saw him shaking his head.

'If the idea of being seen with the cripple is so uncomfortable, we could always call it a departmental staff meeting or something,' he suggested slyly, an extra glimmer of mischief in his eyes. 'Of course, that would mean that it would be a business meeting and I'd be able to get out of paying just so it could go through your accounts.'

'Oh, no, you don't!' she exclaimed, suddenly throwing caution to the winds. She knew exactly what the man thought of her so she was in no danger of being swept off her feet. 'If you vant me to spill my secrets, you vill have to pay!' she ended dramatically in a very bad Eastern European accent.

CHAPTER FOUR

KAT pressed a trembling hand to her stomach, hoping vainly to subdue the butterflies.

'What on earth am I doing?' she demanded in a fierce whisper, all too aware that one or other of her sons could stick their head around the door at any moment.

Now that she thought about it, they probably couldn't remember seeing her get ready to go out for the evening before, so they were hovering, half fascinated and half repelled by the whole spectacle.

'You're painting your *eyes*!' Sam had exclaimed in shock, and she'd been uncomfortably aware that it had been years since she'd done anything more than wash her face and pull a brush through her hair to prepare for her busy days.

Well, Richard had always said that he didn't like seeing women with layers of goop all over their faces, so she supposed she'd taken the easy way out and given up trying. It hadn't been as though she'd needed to wear make-up to attract a man—she had already been married to the kindest one she was likely to meet—and if the conflagration that had erupted on their honeymoon had died down to a comfortable glow, well, she still had the memories of how it had been to keep her warm.

Now she was so out of practice at getting ready to go anywhere that didn't involve entertaining two boys that she didn't know whether she was just setting herself up for another round of ridicule.

She stepped back from the mirror and cast a critical look over herself from head to toe.

Well, she couldn't do much about the shoes because they were the only ones she had that hadn't fallen apart. She couldn't even remember how many years ago she'd bought them. The same thing went for the dress, although that at least was vaguely in fashion, being a basic black with enough softly draped chiffon to hide the fact that she could do with a few more pounds to soften her bony outline. She hadn't realised till now just how much weight she'd lost since Richard had died. Hopefully, some of it would return when she wasn't working flat out all the time.

What she couldn't tell was whether she'd managed to achieve the understated elegance she'd been aiming for or had slipped into over-the-top. It didn't help that she had no idea where the wretched man was taking her.

'Rose…?' she called through the partially open bedroom door, needing another opinion before she lost her nerve and reverted to one of her usual business suits. For a moment she wondered whether her voice had carried over the opening credits of the DVD that was intended to entertain both Rose and the boys. 'Rose, have you got a minute before the film starts?'

She heard a footstep on the polished wood floor in the hallway and her door swung a little wider.

'Rose, tell me what you think...honestly, mind!' she demanded nervously, as she ran her fingers through her freshly washed hair then gave a tug at the side of the dress to make sure it was hanging smoothly. 'Does this look all right or do I look like mutton dressed as lamb?' She held her arms out to turn around and give her volunteer babysitter a look at the finished effect of her efforts...and found Ben standing silently in the doorway.

His eyes were darker than usual as they travelled over her, more the colour of a mysterious forest than sun-dappled emerald, and they were almost fierce by the time they reached her face.

'You look...incredible,' he said softly, his voice huskier than ever.

'Is she ready to go yet?' demanded Sam, his feet pounding along the hallway towards them. 'Mrs Fazackerly won't let us start the film till you've gone.'

'In that case, we'd better go,' said Ben with a smile for the eight-year-old bouncing around with excitement. 'Have you got a wrap or something? The car's warm, but the wind's chilly before you get to it.'

The words were prosaic and their delivery was matter-of-fact, but that couldn't detract from the heated expression in his eyes as they held hers over her son's head.

'Um, I've got a pashmina,' she managed to say, as she reached blindly for the soft violet fabric draped over the back of the chair, chosen to tone with her eye-shadow to heighten the soft grey of her eyes. She wasn't capable of saying anything else, not when his eyes were fixed on her lips like a starving man glimpsing a banquet.

'Let me,' he offered, stepping forward to park his crutches

against her dressing table before he lifted the silky weight of it from her hands to drape it around her shoulders. She shuddered delicately when the tips of his fingers just stroked the bare skin at the back of her neck, marvelling at her reaction to such a tiny contact.

Had she ever responded to Richard like this? she wondered as she watched Ben reclaim the crutches with a white-knuckled grip. She certainly couldn't remember it; could barely remember what her husband had looked like while Ben was standing so close.

She forced herself to look across the room at the photograph sitting beside her bed. She needed to remind herself of the laughing man he'd been on their wedding day as they'd linked arms and drunk to a long and happy future from each other's champagne glasses.

'Mum…!' Sam implored impatiently from the doorway.

'Just you remember to be good for Mrs Fazackerly,' she warned with a fierce frown to make sure he knew she was serious. She'd gone out so seldom that having a sitter was a novelty.

'Course we will,' he declared as he leapt exuberantly onto the other end of the settee, leaving Rose sitting between the two boys. 'We'll be too busy watching the pirates, won't we?' He turned towards the woman gazing avidly up at the two of them, her eyes visibly gleaming at the picture they made together, and Kat barely stopped a groan of resignation.

They weren't going to hear the end of this until Ben left the practice, she realised wryly, even as Sam was urging, 'Go on. Press the button to start. They're going now.'

Josh was silent, but she could see that he was taking everything in, his eyes every bit as serious as his father's had been when he'd been worried about something.

'All right, Josh?' she asked, tightening her hands around her little evening bag as she ached for her elder son's pain. She never should have agreed to go for this meal, not if it was going to hurt him. It wasn't fair.

Then he smiled…a small smile, it was true, but her heart grew instantly lighter that he'd even made the effort.

'You look nice, Mum,' he said quietly, definitely a younger version of his father.

'Thank you, Josh. Now, we won't be back late and you've got our mobile numbers if anything—'

'Oh, pishtosh!' Rose exclaimed impatiently. 'I reared two of my own and I'm not so decrepit that I've forgotten how to do it. Nothing's going to happen except the two of you are going to have a lovely meal. Now scat! We've got a film to watch.'

He'd nearly swallowed his tongue, Ben thought in disbelief as he tried to make it look as if he was ushering Kat out to her car. He'd had a surreptitious practice earlier in the day and had discovered that he could actually fit into the passenger seat if it was pushed all the way back.

It was a struggle, made worse by the fact that he really wasn't concentrating on what he was doing. All he could think about was Kat and the feelings that had swamped him when he'd caught sight of her.

He'd seen her standing there, so elegant and willowy with those layers of filmy fabric drifting around her. Her eyes had been huge and uncertain as she'd turned towards him, thinking he was Rose. Then, when they'd widened still further and her breathing pattern had changed, he'd known with a leap of exultation that she was every bit as affected by him.

And in the mirror behind her he'd been able to see the reflection of her bed…the bed he'd slept in for nearly a week until he hadn't been able to stand being surrounded by her delicate fragrance any more without being able to hold her in his arms and…

And *nothing,* he reminded himself angrily, glad that his groan was hidden by the sound of the engine as she turned the key.

'I'm sorry, did you say something?' she asked, and he saw her glance briefly in his direction. At least, he hoped it had been briefly.

'Sorry. It was nothing,' he muttered, feeling the adolescent heat sear his cheeks as he forced himself to concentrate on anything other than his body's fierce and obvious response to Kat.

The evening hadn't got any better. It seemed that he was doomed to permanent arousal whenever the woman was anywhere near him. All he could hope for was that other people's attention would be drawn to his far-from-elegant crutches. He would hate Kat to be the focus of gossip because he couldn't control his body.

On the other hand, once his lower body was hidden behind a table draped in snowy linen, he could relax enough to enjoy not only the unexpected pleasure of a first-class meal but also a wide-ranging conversation with a woman who had more than her fair share of brains as well as beauty.

It was only when the topics drifted towards the more personal that they both grew more wary.

Kat had no problem at all talking about Josh and the way

he seemed to have retreated into himself after his father's death, or about Sam and his almost obsessive need for order in his little universe.

'Although they both seem to have loosened up a bit recently,' she murmured thoughtfully, and when her grey eyes met his he saw excitement grow. 'Hey, perhaps you're the catalyst!' she exclaimed with a smile that quickly faded. 'It's probably my fault they've been having problems…for not spending enough time with them…giving them a chance to talk things through,' she said sombrely. 'But I had the practice to run and…there was just so much to do after…' She shook her head.

Unfortunately, that was the moment when she decided to turn the spotlight on him.

'So, what about you?' she asked brightly. 'We've been living together… Oops! That didn't come out quite right!' She giggled and he wondered for a moment whether he was going to have to get a taxi to get the two of them home. Then he recalled the way she'd wordlessly put her hand over her glass when the waiter had offered to top it up, and realised it wasn't the wine.

It made him feel good to discover that she was enjoying his company enough to relax. When he'd first met her, she'd been so overwhelmed by her circumstances that she had been strung as tight as piano wire and ready to snap.

'What I *should* have said,' she continued with a hint of a wicked sparkle in her eyes, 'was that we've been sharing the house for exactly two weeks now, and I know nothing more about you than what you told me that first day.'

He had a bad feeling about this conversation. But, then, he always did when it turned in his direction. The reality of his life was so painful that he hadn't been able to work out any simple dismissive words to satisfy idle curiosity, and telling anyone what had really happened just wasn't an option.

'It's also the day when we have to make a decision about my employment,' he pointed out in a moment of inspiration.

'Your employment?' That was definitely a look of panic on her face. 'You mean, you want to *leave*?'

'That's not what I said.' He smiled as warmth spread through him. It might only be because she was desperate not to lose the second doctor in the practice, but he could always stroke his own ego by pretending that it was *him* she wanted to stay. 'If you remember, our original agreement was for an initial two weeks to see whether we worked well together, at which time either of us could call a halt.'

She nodded warily. 'And?' She lobbed the ball straight back into his court.

'And I'm happy to stay on for the rest of the three months, with an option for a further three,' he offered, even as a small voice was shrieking warnings inside his head.

He'd already grown far too close to this little family and staying any longer was a bad idea, but he couldn't in all conscience leave her to be buried under that mountain of responsibilities again—at least, not until she'd found someone reliable to take over from him.

The look of relief and pleasure that spread over her face was like the sun coming up in the dark places inside him, but it also made his misgivings cast deeper shadows.

Kat was an incredibly strong woman but she was also needy, emotionally and practically, and as for her boys... She'd been right in her assessment of the changes that were already evident. Sam was less obsessive now. In fact, he'd been downright bouncy this evening and his infectious giggle was pealing through the house more and more often.

Josh was a harder nut to crack and it would probably take at least the next three months to uncover the reasons for his bouts of sullenness and stubbornness. It could just be the proximity of his teens, but Ben had a feeling that it was far more likely to be connected with his father's illness or his death. If he was lucky, the mere fact that he was a man might persuade Josh to confide in him. Maybe.

'I agree…with reservations,' Kat said suddenly, and for a moment he thought she'd been following his thoughts. Then he remembered they'd been talking about his job.

'Reservations?' It was his turn to be wary.

'If you prove to be an even better GP without your cast as you are limited by it now, I reserve the right to try to persuade you to sign on for a permanent post.'

He managed to laugh and agree that anything was possible, but he knew there really was no chance of that. At least, if he kept moving on, there was little chance of getting too involved in other people's lives. Consequently, there was little chance that they would discover who he was, what he'd been and, most shameful of all, what he'd done.

Regret was a poor bedfellow, but it was the only one he could allow himself for the foreseeable future.

He was heaving himself out of her car under her watchful eye and trying desperately not to remember that this was the point where his much younger self would have been planning how to steal that first goodnight kiss when the original purpose of this evening's outing came back to him.

'So, is this the point where you finally tell me how you

managed to get Mr Aldarini to the head of the appointment queue?' he asked teasingly. 'Did you have to promise the consultant to name your next child after him?'

He cursed his glib tongue when he saw the flash of sorrow, suddenly wondering if she'd wanted more family than her two boys. A girl, perhaps with her soft grey eyes and caring heart?

'Nothing so impossible,' she said quietly. 'It's not really a big secret. Just that I happened to approach the right person at the right time. There's a new broom in the orthopaedic department who's really putting the old guard's backs up about sloppy, wasteful organisation. They say it doesn't need to be changed because that's the way it's always been done, and so the battle rages.'

'And in the meantime?' he prompted, leaning one shoulder against the door frame while she found the right key.

'In the meantime, I phoned up and told his secretary that my patient was in a bad way and he immediately suggested shoe-horning him in during his outpatient clinic tomorrow morning so he can start the process going…the X-rays, bloods and so on. I also told his secretary to make a note that Mr Aldarini would be willing to be called in at short notice, in case another patient was deemed inoperable for some reason, and left a gap in the schedule.'

'No one expects the common cold to disrupt something as important as a long-awaited operation, but it happens,' Ben agreed, remembering the number of times he'd seen just that. 'And the more life-threatening the operation is, the more important it is that the patient is otherwise fit and healthy.'

Kat's face was sweetly serious as she listened to him, the light falling through the glass panel in the door falling over her smooth skin and outlining the slender nose and unexpectedly stubborn chin while throwing her eyes into deeper shadow. And in spite of the fact he was trying to concentrate on anything *but* the desire to taste those smiling lips, all he could think of…all he wanted…was to throw caution to the winds and take her in his arms.

If only he could, he thought grimly, forcing his eyes away from her.

'Watch your crutches on the doorstep,' she reminded him prosaically as she stepped into the warmth of the hallway, and the moment was gone. Not that it was ever likely to happen, with him on crutches and Kat as busy as a one-armed paperhanger *and* with two children in the house.

And he really didn't need to be sacked for inappropriate behaviour towards his boss, he thought grimly, angry that he'd even been thinking about crossing that line.

What was it about Kat Leeman that had started the block of ice around his heart melting? She was a widow…a mother of two boys…and all three of them were still having problems coming to terms with the loss of a husband and father. He certainly wasn't the person to help them, not with his track record. He'd barely noticed when Lorraine had complained of headaches, knowing how stressful her job had been. If he'd been more caring…

'Goodnight, Ben,' she called softly on her way into the sitting room. 'I'll just go and drop Rose back home then I'll lock up.'

Frustration that she was having to do a job that should have been his made him thump the hateful crutches down much harder than he should have and he paused momentarily by the boys' bedroom door to make certain that he hadn't woken them.

Except Josh obviously hadn't been to sleep yet, the tired eyes meeting his so watchfully from between the rails of the top bunk telling him that he'd been determined to make sure his mother returned safely.

'All right?' he asked softly, and received a silent nod in reply.

'Did you enjoy the film?' This time there was the hint of a smile, but Ben could tell that there was definitely something on the boy's mind. Suddenly he knew exactly what it was, but it took him a moment to find the words to put his fears to rest.

'Well, your mum will probably tell you that we had a lovely meal, in spite of the fact we were talking shop all evening.' With his hands occupied with the crutches it would be difficult to cross his fingers, but he could imagine himself doing it in the hope that Josh would bite.

'Shop?' A tiny frown appeared on that smooth forehead, and Ben sent up a silent cheer.

'Oh.' He chuckled softly. 'That's what you call it when you're only talking about business all the time. You have to be on your toes when you're having a meal with your boss.'

He almost saw the tension drain out of those thin shoulders and then the tousled head settled itself more comfortably on the pillow. 'I wouldn't want to talk *shop* if I was having a meal in a restaurant,' he said with a sleepy yawn. 'I'd be *eating*…'

Ben turned away and came face to face with Kat.

He was shocked to see the gleam of tears in her eyes.

'Thank you,' she whispered almost soundlessly. 'I hadn't realised that he might think…might be worrying…' She shook her head when she couldn't find the words to voice her concerns, instead volunteering, 'They idolised Richard, even though he didn't have much time free to spend with them. Even a knockabout with a football…'

'Shh. It's all right. I understand,' he murmured, and stepped aside to allow her to look in on the boys. He was turning to make his way up the spiral staircase to his domain, only to catch sight of Rose hovering in the sitting room doorway with an ominously thoughtful expression on her face.

Kat couldn't being herself to meet Ben's eyes at breakfast the next morning.

Ordinarily, the conversation at the table was a cheerful combination of chat and chivvying, with the boys seeming to enjoy the fact that Ben had continued to join them in spite of the fact that he'd now moved upstairs.

Until this morning Kat had taken pleasure in his presence, too, feeling that the addition of an adult male voice to the usual mixture had made the sound somehow more complete. Now…

Now all she could think about was the fact that she hadn't been able to take her eyes off him all evening, excruciatingly aware of every movement he'd made and every word he'd said.

By the time they'd been standing on the front step, with Ben waiting for her to find the key, she'd actually convinced herself that he was going to end the evening in the traditional way between men and women…with a kiss. Then he'd looked away, almost glaring at the front door as though desperate to get inside and away from her.

This morning was just as bad, with his concentration totally on Josh and Sam, no matter how inane the topic. In fact, the sooner the boys went to school, the better. Once she was sitting in her room, behind her desk, her world would be back under control again and she…

Her train of thought was so eerily similar to her description of Sam's reaction to losing his father that it brought her up sharp.

What on earth was going on here? she demanded silently. She *had* come to terms with losing Richard. It had been an absolute necessity if she was going to be able to keep the practice running and a roof over their heads.

Well, if that was the case, she continued as she tried to prepare for the first patient of the day, why was she feeling so guilty because she'd *wanted* Ben to kiss her?

'Ooh! My head's in such a muddle!' she groaned aloud in exasperation, flinging her hands in the air. Luckily, the neat stack of patient notes didn't go flying. 'I'm attracted to him, but I feel guilty about it…' Especially as she'd never felt this much sexual attraction to anyone before—not even Richard.

'I trust him with the patients…with my *sons*, for heaven's sake, but I have no idea even if he's married.' He didn't wear a ring but, then, many men didn't, especially in their profession. 'He avoids answering questions…as though he has something to hide…'

She said the words aloud and cringed, because it sounded as though she was accusing him of hiding a dark secret. In fact, nothing could be further from the truth. She could tell from the pain in his eyes that something was eating at him inside, destroying his pleasure in his job and in his relationships with other people.

She laughed wryly, recognising some of the traits she'd taken notes on during those long-ago basic psychology lectures.

'And I've been just as guilty,' she admitted, recognising the way she'd been keeping the rest of the world at arm's length while she'd tried to make sense of her life without Richard.

It had taken Ben's arrival to wake her hormones up and remind her that she was still a young woman. Unfortunately, it looked as if she was still a one-man woman. The first time it had been Richard, but this time it looked as if her heart had chosen the unattainable—Ben.

'Good morning, Melissa,' she said as a petite youngster came in. 'Sit down and make yourself comfortable while we wait for your grandmother to come in.' It was well known in Ditchling that the elderly couple had taken on the care of their granddaughter several years ago when her parents had been killed during a freak storm on holiday.

'Um, actually, Doctor, she doesn't know I'm here. Some of the teachers have to go on a professional development course so we got the day off, only I didn't tell my nan, so she thinks I'm at school as usual.' She looked up from her contemplation of her school uniform skirt with a worried expression. 'Is that a problem? Does she have to be here with me because I'm only twelve—well, nearly twelve, anyway?'

'Well…' Kat was caught in a difficult position here, but the poor child obviously wanted to talk to someone, so perhaps she could take a chance and stretch the rules. 'Legally, I can't examine you or do any tests without a responsible adult as your guardian. But if you just wanted to have a bit of a chat about something that's worrying you…?'

'Yes, please,' she whispered, tilting her head forward again so that a silky curtain of toffee-coloured hair all but hid her face. 'I've got no one I can talk to about…about girl things. You know?'

Kat smiled encouragingly, wondering just what was coming. Surely Melissa was far too young to be enquiring about contraception, but maybe that was preferable to an unwanted pregnancy or even a life-threatening disease?

'And you can't talk to your friends or a teacher?'

'No!' She looked horrified. 'I don't know any of them, not really. I only went up to the big school this term and…'

'And you don't want to say anything that people might gossip about?'

'Exactly!' she said, clearly relieved that Kat understood.

'So, what is it you wanted to talk about? Boys? Periods? Kissing? Bras? Tampons?' She threw out a list of the more universal topics that came up when she was speaking to young teens.

'None of those, exactly. It's…well, it's embarrassing but…' She was clearly having a problem screwing her courage up but Kat was happy to wait. It could save an awful lot of problems further down the line if she fostered a good relationship with the youngster this early on.

'I think there's something wrong with me,' she burst out suddenly, her cheeks almost scarlet with mortification. 'I'm wet…down there…all the time!'

Kat smiled, partly to reassure the girl but mostly in relief that it was such a simple problem.

'Of course you are!' she exclaimed, adding matter-of-factly, 'If you weren't, you'd squeak when you walked.'

Kat saw the pretty blue eyes grow wide and the childish mouth open in surprise and then she giggled. 'S-squeak?' she repeated through her laughter.

'Well, it would definitely be very uncomfortable,' Kat confirmed with a chuckle of her own. It was easy, then, to ask a few pertinent questions to eliminate the possibility of idiopathic genito-urinary infections, and within a matter of minutes Melissa's worries were completely put to rest.

'Thank you so much,' she said politely as she hopped down from the chair, a positive spring in her step.

'There was probably a lot going on in the first days in your new school, but you'll probably find that there's a school nurse who you could have gone to for a chat,' Kat told her as she ushered her towards the door. 'But, by all means, get in contact if you have any further worries.'

'Thank you, Doctor.' She paused, her head on one side while she pondered something. 'Do people *really* come to you asking about kissing?' she demanded, and Kat laughed and sent her on her way.

CHAPTER FIVE

THAT evening, having managed very successfully to avoid being alone with Ben all day, Kat had every intention of keeping her distance from him at home, too.

In her head, she was just lining up all the overdue jobs—such as the hated ironing pile—and was actually crossing her fingers for a busy series of call-outs when she heard shouts from the small patch of lawn in the back garden and went to explore.

The sight that met her eyes was one that she couldn't have imagined of the austere-looking man she'd interviewed just two weeks ago as he sprawled full-length on the ground with her two boys sitting on him. All three males were covered in mud after the recent rain, and the filthy state of Ben's cast gave her severe concern for the state of the healing bone inside it.

But she didn't think she'd ever seen Josh and Sam look quite so happy as they clung on fiercely to stop Ben from reaching the ball.

'Hey! What are you doing over there?' Ben called, when he caught sight of her leaning against the corner of the house. 'Come and rescue me!'

'Yeah, Mum, come and join in,' Sam invited eagerly.

'In my work suit? I don't think so,' she said with a laugh. 'Anyway, I think there's far too much testosterone over there for a woman's safety. I'll stay over here and be the referee.'

A bell began ringing beside her and she recognised the timer from the kitchen.

'End of the match,' Ben announced, looking across at Kat. 'So tell us, referee, who's the winner?'

'That depends whether we're counting goals or tons of mud per body,' she said dryly, as her two stood up and she got her first good look at the damage. 'I didn't see any goals, so... Ben, where are your crutches?' she demanded as he began to struggle like an upturned beetle.

'One of them's leaning against the side of the house and the other one's here...' He dug around under his hip and un-earthed the muddy object.

'Right, boys...get yourselves inside, strip off your outer clothing and leave it in the corner of the kitchen beside the washing machine and scoot into the bathroom. You both need a shower...and a hair wash before you eat, so hurry up!'

'OK!' chirped Sam, and began sprinting towards the door.

'Mum...?' Josh lingered with a look of concern on his face that was totally out of keeping for an eleven-year-old. 'You're not going to tell him off, are you? It's our fault he got all muddy. He was only going to tell us what to do and then...'

'No, Josh, I'm not going to tell him off because I know exactly who to blame for this. Me! For encouraging you to play football in the first place. Now scoot, and keep an eye on Sam so he doesn't flood the bathroom floor again.'

She saw the grin on his face as he loped after his little brother and sighed with relief at having sorted one problem.

Now for the much bigger one, she thought as she retrieved the second crutch.

'You shouldn't have been doing this, Ben,' she said quietly, as she walked across the muddy patch that used to be a lawn, just in case Josh had lingered to listen. 'You could have done your leg some real damage.'

'I could have if I'd really been fighting with them, or if I'd tried to kick the ball,' he agreed, looking up at her as she offered a hand to help pull him up off the ground. He looked from her slender clean fingers to his much larger, infinitely dirtier ones and chuckled. 'Are you sure you really want to do this?'

'Come on. Give me your hand and use the other crutch to help lever yourself up. How heavily did you fall?' she demanded, as he made light work of the manoeuvre, surprisingly strong and limber in spite of the ungainly cast.

'I didn't actually fall at all,' he explained in a low voice with a quick glance towards the house. 'It was more of a tuck and roll for the boys' benefit. I just wasn't expecting the grass to be so wet and slippery.'

'The drainage isn't very good on this side of the house so it gets very muddy. That's another job on the list of many that we…*I* haven't got around to yet.'

Suddenly it was as if Richard's ghost was standing between them, so she wasn't surprised when Ben said, 'Tell me about your husband.'

'Richard?' She played for time, wondering exactly what he wanted to know.

'I presume there hasn't been a cast of thousands,' he teased, as he lumbered gingerly across the muddy terrain until he reached the paving by a rather tired-looking wooden bench and cautiously lowered himself onto one end of it, apparently prepared to wait for whatever she wanted to tell him.

'We met while we were both at med school,' she said with a reminiscent smile, 'and married a month after I qualified. We already had the boys by the time we came to Ditchling. Dr Fraser was ready to retire. He'd been struggling to keep up with the demands of the practice for several years since his wife had had her stroke. All he wanted was to take her to live in Spain so she could swim every day and sit in the warmth of the sun.' She'd been so inspired to see the deep love between the older couple at first hand and delighted to hear, later, that Nora Fraser had taken on a whole new lease of life with their move to a warmer climate.

She cast her eyes up at the overcast sky and pulled a face.

'I can't imagine why,' Ben deadpanned. 'So what sort of state *was* the practice in?'

'It was hard going,' she admitted bluntly. 'He'd only been going through the motions so it was very run-down. People had started drifting away because they could never be sure that the practice would be open when they arrived. They'd been signing on with other practices or they were just going to the hospital.'

'Well, it's certainly thriving now. How did you turn it around?' he demanded, the praise warming her in spite of the chilly breeze that had sprung up.

Kat suddenly realised that it was nice sitting here with Ben, in spite of the discomfort of delving into her memories. It felt good to be having a conversation with someone who wasn't either a patient or a half-pint size asking for help with homework or wanting to know what was on the menu for supper.

'We bit the bullet and sank money we didn't have into re-vamping the front—painting the façade of the house, widening the driveway and paving it for off-road parking—and every night, once the boys were in bed, we spent endless hours redecorating the inside.' She felt exhausted just re-membering that time.

'We couldn't afford to alienate the few patients we had left so the practice had to remain open all the way through the work, but we decided we ought to have a grand re-opening.' She laughed briefly. 'It caused barely a ripple and the patient numbers hardly changed. Richard was almost in despair when the area was hit by a flu epidemic, followed by a gastric bug, followed by an outbreak of chickenpox in a couple of the local schools…bang, bang, bang, one after the other… And, in no time we were being rushed off our feet. And of course, with more patients on our books, our funding went up and we could finally stop worrying about everything col-lapsing around us.'

Looking back, she could see that those had been the days when they'd achieved everything they'd ever hoped for, if only they'd had the time to enjoy it.

'Then, out of the blue, Richard fell ill and it was like history repeating itself. Just like Dr Fraser with his wife, I was spending every moment I could with Richard. All I could concentrate on was the fact that he was already so ill when the diagnosis was made that they were having to hit the leukaemia with the chemo really aggressively. The drugs were very powerful and they made him so…'

She shook her head, unable to meet his eyes after one swift glimpse of the sympathy in them for fear she'd lose a year's worth of hard-won control.

'He never really had a chance of beating it,' she whispered, saying aloud the words she'd used to console herself for the last year. 'Apart from anything else, he didn't have any reserves, after exhausting himself like that to get the practice up and running…' She continued the litany, surprised that this time the ache of loss was duller than before. Was it true that time made things easier to bear? Or was it something about the tacit support she felt emanating from the silent figure beside her? Or was it that she was finally ready to admit something that she'd had to suppress into a deep, dark corner inside her—something that had made her so angry that she just hadn't been able to cope with it at the time.

She raised her head and deliberately met those amazing green eyes as she voiced the unthinkable. 'The boys and I needed him but Richard wasn't interested. Once he heard the diagnosis, he just…gave up.'

It took a moment for her to realise that Ben wasn't looking at her so much as through her, and she realised she'd just made a monumental mistake, pouring her heart out to someone who wasn't really interested in her petty—

'Sometimes it's the only way they can cope with it,' Ben said suddenly, his husky voice as rough as a mile of gravelled road.

'Pardon?' She'd been so overwhelmed with embarrassment at making such a fool of herself that she didn't understand what he was saying.

'I mean, when a patient gets that sort of diagnosis…particularly one of the cancers…it seems as if it either switches them into fight mode, and they battle with everything they've got, or they switch off.'

'Exactly!' she agreed. 'I've seen both responses, over and over again, but Richard had always been such a fighter…like the way he worked himself to a standstill to make the practice a success. I just couldn't believe the way he just seemed to—'

'Sometimes,' Ben interrupted slowly, thoughtfully, that far-away look in his eyes again as he tried to put those thoughts into words. 'Sometimes I think they just *know* that it's a battle they can't win.'

'But…' she began, only to have his expression still her objections unspoken. Even his eyes seemed dulled with the weight of his thoughts and suddenly she realised that he wasn't just speaking theoretically. This was something that had touched him, personally.

She was trying to find the words to ask if it had been his wife he'd lost when he began speaking again, and the moment was lost because she didn't want to miss a word.

'It's almost as if…as if they deliberately switch off all the fighting mechanisms because they want the inevitable to be over as soon as possible…as if they realise that fighting will only *delay* the inevitable, not prevent it. That the false hope will actually make it worse than ever in the long run, so, for the sake of the people they're leaving behind, they just…let go.'

It was such a simple explanation that she couldn't see why she hadn't thought of it for herself. It was certainly a far more acceptable reason for why Richard had gone so fast…far better than that he just hadn't cared enough to try…that she and the boys hadn't been important enough to him…

'I hadn't looked at it like that before,' she said, as a feeling of peace stole over her. 'And it was exactly the sort of reasoning Richard *would* have used, especially when you think of how hard we'd had to work to rescue the practice from the effects of Nora Fraser's illness.'

'Mum!' The childish voice came floating out of the

window towards them. 'Sam's using up all the shampoo. There won't be any left for me…'

Kat grinned, the introspective mood completely shattered. And she'd never had the chance to ask him who he'd been talking about when he'd said—

'*And* he's getting all the towels wet!' Josh added in tones of disgust, and she sighed.

'Back to being a referee,' she said as she stood and automatically held out her hand to help him to his feet.

'I hadn't realised how dirty my hands were when you helped me up before,' he said apologetically, holding them up, palms outward, for her inspection.

'Mine aren't made of sugar…they'll wash,' she said with a dismissive shrug, grasping each of them in hers and leaning back to give herself some leverage.

The job was far easier than she expected and suddenly there he was right in front of her so that her nose was practically pressed against his mud-streaked sweatshirt.

He made no move to step back, probably because he had nowhere to go with the bench behind him, while she seemed incapable of moving at all, totally wrapped up in the way every one of her senses was responding to his proximity.

She was just about to add the stimulus of the sense of touch, her hand venturing up to brush away the crumbs of soil clinging to the embroidered logo over his heart, when there were the simultaneous sounds of a heavy thud and something crashing, followed by Josh's bellow.

'Mum! Sam's fallen! He's bleeding!'

Kat was never certain how she got there so fast—she had no memory of running across the garden into the house or through her bedroom into the bathroom. The enduring image burned into her mind was of her younger son sitting on the bathroom floor surrounded by a seeping pool of expensive green bath oil explosively released from its glass bottle while blood dripped freely from a gash on his arm.

'I should have stopped him, Mum,' Josh said shakily, his face completely white. 'He was standing on the edge of the bath to look into the mirror and he just fell.' And knocked over Richard's last gift to her in the process, she noted sadly, but that was hardly the most important matter.

'Don't move, either of you,' she ordered. 'There's glass on the floor and you've both got bare feet.'

'I'll take care of Josh,' said a deep voice, and she realised for the first time that Ben had followed her in her headlong dash. 'You have a look and see what Sam's done to himself.'

It took several seconds for her to organise her thoughts…seconds in which she saw Ben effortlessly lift Josh off his feet one-handed, directing him to grab a couple of towels off the rail before he hobbled heavily out of the bathroom. One towel was dropped on the carpet just inside her bedroom before he lowered Josh onto it, wrapping him firmly in the other.

Then her concentration was focused solely on the naked body huddled on the floor in front of her, her emotions tangling with her professionalism so that she was uncertain just what to do for him first.

'Can you get him into the shower to wash that gunk off him, or do you want me to do it?' Ben prompted, but somehow just the sound of his voice had steadied her and set her mind working properly again.

'I can manage,' she said firmly, suiting her actions to her

words and reaching round the shower screen to set the water running. 'Have you hurt yourself anywhere else, Sam?' she asked as she played the shower nozzle over him, working steadily from head to foot. So far, all she could see was the wound on his arm, but there was still a thick layer of bath oil on his lower body.

'Just my head,' he mumbled, his voice strangely slurred. 'My head hurts.'

'Did you hit it when you fell?' Her anxious fingers returned to search for bumps and cuts or, worst of all, indentations. She sighed with relief when nothing was immediately obvious.

'Don't know. Don't think so,' he said shortly, as though speaking was too much effort to bother with anything further.

'Any LoC?' Ben prompted from the doorway, but it was Josh who answered.

'No,' he said firmly, serious beyond his years. 'I know LoC means loss of consciousness. I read it in one of Dad's books. Sam didn't knock himself out but he was sort of…*not there* for a moment, as if he was dizzy.'

'Good observation, Josh. Very helpful,' Ben praised generously, and Kat suddenly realised that *she* should have been the one to do it. Josh was her son and she should have realised that he needed reassurance after such an accident. He worried too much as it was, almost hovering over her and Sam as though…

The sudden revelation was almost blinding in its obviousness. Why hadn't she realised that, with his father gone, Josh had assumed that it was *his* job to watch out for them?

Had she been walking around with her eyes closed for the last year? Why hadn't she recognised Josh's withdrawal into himself as something more than the impending advent of his teens?

'Sit down a minute, Josh,' Ben said, but though his voice was calm, there was something in his tone that made Kat glance swiftly in their direction.

Josh was looking paler than ever, in spite of the fact that Sam didn't seem to be badly injured. The cut was so neat and clean that it would probably take little more than a few stitches to repair the damage to his arm, but Josh was looking distinctly wobbly.

'Come on, old son. Down you go,' Ben urged, just managing to catch him when he would have crumpled.

'Is it just shock?' Kat called softly, not wanting to frighten Sam, although it was time to take him out of the shower now, so he would soon see that Josh was lying down on the floor inside her bedroom.

'That, and a cut under his foot,' Ben confirmed grimly. 'He must have stood on a piece of glass when he went to help his brother.'

'How bad is it?' Kat was torn between her boys, but she didn't have enough hands to help them both.

'He'll need stitches,' Ben said matter-of-factly. 'It'll be sore, but definitely not life-threatening. How about Sam?'

'The same,' she said on a wave of relief that things hadn't been much worse. She turned off the water and reached for a couple of towels, choosing the oldest one to bind Sam's arm before wrapping him warmly in the other one. 'I'm going to carry him through to the kitchen.'

'I'll follow you through in a minute with Josh,' Ben confirmed, as he moved aside to let her squeeze past him in the doorway. 'Have you got everything necessary to take care of them in the house or will you need me to fetch things from the surgery?'

'I can't remember,' she admitted uncertainly, suddenly glad for the reassuring presence of another adult while she dealt with this family crisis. She felt a swift surge of rage towards Richard simply for not being here when she needed him, then forced herself to shut the feeling away where it could do no harm.

Josh and Sam were here and they needed her. Ben was willing to help. The rest was wasted energy.

'Neither of them gets hurt very often and they usually don't need much more than a wash and a dab of antiseptic covered by a dressing,' she explained, as she set off across her bedroom and out into the hallway, leaving Ben with his hand on Josh's shoulder as though persuading him to lie still for a moment.

'Sit up here, sweetheart,' Kat said, as she deposited Sam on the work surface beside the sink. 'Are you still feeling dizzy?'

'No. Just… My head hurts… And my arm…'

OK. Straightforward injuries she could cope with without falling apart, she told herself sternly as she opened the cupboard and pulled out the first-aid box that Richard had insisted she keep there.

Now that she thought about it, she couldn't remember the thing actually being opened since he died, and that wasn't good. A house with two boys in it, an eight-year-old and an eleven-year-old, ought to be using adhesive dressings on a regular basis if they were up to all the usual things that boys of their age did.

A quick flick through the contents steadied her hands for the task ahead and told her there were most of the things she needed to get on with patching up the boys' injuries.

'What do we need?' Ben asked, already carrying Josh into

the room to settle him on one of the chairs. At least he had a little more colour in his cheeks now.

'Just sutures, I think,' she said, dreading the next few minutes. It was so hard knowing that you were going to have to inflict pain on your child, even temporarily.

'I'll go round to the surgery to get them,' he offered, then threw her an unexpected grin. 'Don't start without me!' he admonished, before hurrying away.

'Right, Sam,' Kat began, already missing Ben's steadying presence in the room. 'I'm going to need to give that cut a last wash out with the squirty nozzle on this special bottled water and then I'll be able to stop it bleeding, but first I'm going to need to put some medicine around the cut so it won't hurt you. OK?'

'The medicine won't make me sick, will it…like Daddy?' Her heart clenched and for a moment she couldn't even breathe.

'No, sweetheart. It's a different sort of medicine altogether,' she said, wrapping both arms around him as she fought off the urge to cry.

'Promise?' His eyes were so like his father's as they gazed up at her.

'I promise,' she said, and when he closed his eyes, she closed hers for a moment, too, praying for concentration so that she could ignore the fact that this was her *son* she was about to treat.

She picked up the syringe and could hardly focus on the tip of the needle because it was trembling so much.

'May I?' asked Ben's husky voice. She hadn't even heard him return, and when she saw his rock-steady hand held out to take the syringe from her, the relief nearly buckled her knees.

'Please. Be my guest,' she said shakily, and he grinned at her.

'I think I already am,' he pointed out, as he donned disposable gloves from the packet in the kit with the speed and ease of long practice. 'So, tell me, Sam,' he continued conversationally, 'what were you trying to do when you climbed on the side of the bath?'

'Wanted to see myself…in the big mirror,' he said, apparently unaware that Ben was swiftly infiltrating the edges of the cut with analgesic. 'It's too high.'

Guilt hit Kat in a broadside. How long had she been promising to put a mirror over the basin for the boys? Probably ever since they'd grown out of the little step-up they'd used when they'd been learning to use the toilet. If she'd only found a handyman to do it for her, she wouldn't have two injured sons.

'What'cha doing?' Josh asked from his position at the kitchen table, his injured foot propped up on a second chair, effectively immobilising him as well as preventing him from seeing what was happening to his little brother.

'I'm going to put some stitches in Sam's arm so it'll heal faster,' Ben explained simply. 'Then I'll do the same for you in your foot.'

'Isn't Mum going to do it?' Josh asked nervously.

'Not this time, sport,' Ben said easily. 'Your mum's never seen my needlework so I thought it was time she saw how good I am at putting people back together.'

Kat marvelled that he could keep up a stream of inconsequential chatter to relax the boys while he was waiting for the analgesia to work. The conversation didn't even pause when he gestured for Kat to irrigate the wound while he held the edges open, or when he put in what must have been the swiftest, neatest row of sutures she'd ever seen.

'OK, sport. That's you finished,' he announced, straightening up and stripping off his gloves as though the gesture was second nature to him. 'Your mum will just put a dressing over it to stop you getting any supper in it, and it can start getting better.'

'Did it hurt, Sam?' Josh asked warily, knowing it was his turn now.

'Just in my head,' Sam said tearfully. 'I wish Dr Ben could make that hurt go away, too.'

'But your arm doesn't hurt any more?' Josh persisted, as Kat carried Sam across and settled him into the comfortable armchair that sat in the corner to take advantage of the view out into the garden and beyond.

'Nah!' Sam said, as he curled up under the blanket Kat tucked around him. 'It's OK, Josh. Honest.'

'Ready, Josh?' Ben said with a smile, and Kat was fighting tears again when she saw her son bite his lip nervously even as he nodded. 'So, you've been reading your dad's books, have you?' he asked, as he settled the eleven-year-old up on the counter with his foot hanging over the sink.

'Some of them,' Josh admitted, with a guilty glance in Kat's direction. 'I was very careful not to spoil them, but some of them have got very big words in them.'

'I know!' Ben exclaimed with a laugh. 'And some very gory pictures, too.'

'Yeah!' Josh pulled a face. 'The one I like best is the first-aid one, cos that's got some of the stuff we learned about in school…about what to do if someone has a neppy-something fit.'

'Epileptic?' Ben suggested, as he pulled on a fresh pair of gloves and reached for a new syringe.

'That's it,' Josh agreed, apparently so interested in what he was telling Ben that he barely more than winced and sucked air through his teeth as the injections went into his foot. 'There's someone in my class who's got it, but he's on tablets and doesn't have fits any more so he's just like the rest of us.'

'What else did they tell you about first aid?' Ben prompted, leaning casually against the edge of the worktop while he waited for the analgesia to do its work.

'About ABC…and the recovery position,' Josh said, then explained confidently, 'That's airway, breathing and circulation, to make sure the person's alive, and the recovery position if the ABC is OK, so they're still all right when the ambulance gets there. But I didn't need to do any of that with Sam because he wasn't unconscious. And, anyway, I couldn't get near him to do it because of the glass.'

By that time, Ben had enlisted Kat's assistance to position Josh's foot so that he could probe the injury for any residual fragments of glass, but a thorough cleaning with a vigorous squirt of saline put both their minds at rest.

Then, once again, it was time to marvel at Ben's fantastic suturing technique, the knotting process so fast and accurate that she could hardly see exactly how he did it.

There were fewer stitches this time, Josh's injury being deep rather than long, and then it was time for the adhesive dressing.

'Right, guys. No getting those bandages wet for the next couple of days,' Ben decreed. 'And let your mum or me know if the cut gets more painful so we can check up on it.'

'In case it gets infected,' Josh threw in with a knowledge-able nod.

'Exactly,' Ben agreed, with a smile that completely dispelled the memory of the sombre expression he'd worn when Kat had first met him. 'You really know your stuff, young Leeman. Are you thinking of becoming a doctor?'

'Like my dad,' Josh said so seriously that it immediately raised a warning flag in Kat's mind.

To have her son choose to be a doctor because it was what he really wanted to do was one thing, but to set himself off on that exhausting treadmill just because the father he'd lost had been a doctor...that could spell disaster.

'And do you know whether your tetanus injections are up to date?' Ben continued with barely a pause, but Kat had a feeling that he'd picked up on exactly the same unnerving intensity that she had.

'I'm not sure,' Josh said with a frown. 'Mum, have we had tetanus injections?'

'Everything's all right, Josh. You won't get lockjaw... although that might be one way of getting a bit of peace around here.' She glanced across at Sam, surprised that he wasn't bouncing back as quickly as she'd expected. The analgesia should have taken away all the pain from his injury, but he was still huddled under the blanket in the corner of the chair.

'Hey, Sam?' she said softly. 'Do you want to put your pyjamas on before supper?' She reached out to smooth his hair away from his forehead then snatched it back when he moaned and knocked it away irritably.

'Don't touch me, please...it hurts,' he moaned.

'What hurts, sweetheart? Your arm?' She glanced across at Ben to find him watching Sam's reaction.

'My head,' Sam moaned, fending her off when she would have smoothed his forehead again. 'Mum…' Then he leaned over the arm of the chair and was sick on the floor.

CHAPTER SIX

'It's probably just a reaction to cutting himself and having stitches,' Ben soothed. 'We've both checked his head for bumps and bruises and there's absolutely no evidence of concussion.'

It had been an hour before Kat finally allowed him to drag her away from Sam's bedside.

'I know that,' she admitted. 'It's just…'

'It's just that he's your baby and you hate the thought that he's hurt and you want to guard him like a mother lion in case anything worse comes along,' he finished for her, and she had to smile.

'Got it in one,' she agreed. 'And he did seem to feel much better after he'd been sick.'

'Look on the bright side. It's the weekend and he'll be right as rain by Monday and itching to tell his classmates all about it.'

Kat groaned. 'And exaggerate like mad. I'll probably have to explain the real story next time I go to a parent-teacher meeting, just to set things straight. But in the meantime, I'm going to see if I can find a handyman of some sort to get that mirror put up, then he won't be tempted to go mountaineering again.'

'You've already got the mirror?'

'That's the most annoying part about the whole episode,' she admitted. 'We bought the wretched thing nearly two years ago and Richard never got around to doing anything about it. And since he died…'

'You've hardly had time to breathe in the last year, Kat, let alone finish off DIY projects. Give yourself *some* credit,' he argued, and she realised uncomfortably that he was reasoning with her almost as if she were one of the boys. 'You've had too many balls up in the air and you've been juggling like mad to keep them there,' he continued. 'If this is the only one you've dropped and the only fallout is a couple of sets of stitches…well, I think you're amazing!'

His unexpected praise was like balm to her soul and certainly didn't sound as if he saw her as a child, but it still caused her to blush like a teenager…something she hadn't done for years. In fact, she couldn't remember how many years it had been since someone had made her blush, especially someone like Ben. He was the epitome of tall, dark and handsome, with more than a touch of the mean, moody and magnificent about him…except delete the *mean*, she corrected silently, because that definitely wasn't part of his character, not if his rough-and-tumble football match with the boys was anything to go by or his deft handling of their injuries.

'So,' he began again when she couldn't find any words, her thoughts too private to voice, 'was there any of the chilli con carne left?'

'Lots,' she confirmed, glad of the change of topic. 'If you remember, I gave Sam scrambled egg for his supper instead, in case the spices were too much for his stomach—'

'Much to his disgust,' he threw in with a grin.

'And Josh's appetite wasn't really up to much either,' she added.

'I got the feeling that he was worried that the whole thing was his fault,' Ben suggested diffidently, as he served himself another plateful, almost as though he was testing the waters to see how she would react.

Kat smiled wryly that his thoughts had mirrored her own. 'As though *he* should somehow have been able to prevent it,' she agreed, watching him put the plate in the microwave and press buttons. 'But that's the whole thing about accidents… they're accidental! They're not anyone's fault…except maybe mine for not getting that stupid mirror put up.'

'So, what sort of tools have you got on hand?' Ben asked conversationally, as he settled himself at the table and forked up a mouthful of steaming food. 'An electric drill? A screwdriver? If you've got those, I could probably get the thing put up in a matter of minutes.'

'Oh, but I can't ask you to do that,' she exclaimed, guilt seizing her once again. He already did far too much for her, including keeping an ear out for the boys when she was called out at night.

'You didn't ask. I offered,' he said firmly. 'So if you get everything together tomorrow morning, I'll do it at the end of morning surgery. The boys can help me, if they'd like.'

It was that last sentence that demolished all her objections. Both Josh and Sam had loved 'helping' Richard on the odd occasions when he'd been doing something like mowing the lawn or washing the car…not that those events had happened very often, she had to admit. She'd ended up being in charge of the lawnmower to make certain the area around the practice looked neat and welcoming, and Richard had begun taking the car through the carwash when it had been installed at the local petrol station to save time.

'Provided you have an inexhaustible supply of patience with boys who over-use the word *why*, I'd be very grateful,' she conceded. 'You probably noticed from their reaction to you in the garden earlier that they've been rather starved of male attention.'

'No grandparents or uncles handy?' he prompted casually.

'We were both only children, so there are no handy siblings around. Richard's parents died before I met him and mine moved out to Cyprus when their arthritis got bad. Dad was stationed there when he was in the armed forces and loved it and the people, so when they got the chance to go back…'

'Has the move been good for them?' He was already halfway through the food, his appetite much better than in the first few days he'd been with them. Then it had almost seemed as if he wasn't really interested in what he put in his mouth. Perhaps sharing meals with two boys who inhaled anything put in front of them had made the difference.

'Health-wise, it's definitely been good. It's given them a new lease on life. They're swimming every day and walking more and more, and they've already built up a large circle of friends, and their social life…well! It's hard to catch them home.' And she'd been fighting an unreasonable jealousy that they hadn't thought twice about staying closer to help her with the boys once the idea of emigrating had come up. So she'd felt duty bound to reassure them that she was coping very well by herself.

'But?'

'There's always a *but,* isn't there?' She chuckled, resigned to keeping her selfish thoughts to herself. 'Whenever I *do* speak to them, they complain that they're missing seeing the boys grow up. They were hoping that once Richard and I got the practice on its feet, we would be able to start going out there for regular visits, holidays and so on, but…with one thing and another, there just hasn't been the time or the money so far.'

She also had the sneaking suspicion that Richard had resented her closeness to her parents, having had to get used to the fact that his had died while he'd still been training.

Of course it had been important to get the practice looking good and running well, but they could both have done with a break before they'd started remodelling their own living space, surely. Perhaps, if he hadn't been so exhausted, Richard might have noticed the symptoms of his leukaemia soon enough for it to have been treated. Perhaps he might never have been struck by it at all…

The phone rang, mercifully dragging her away from that self-destructive thought.

'Ditchling Surger—'

'Please, Doctor, you've got to come. His chest hurts and all down one arm and he says it's difficult to breathe. I think he's had a heart attack!' interrupted the frantic voice on the other end of the phone.

'Have you phoned for an ambulance?' Kat demanded, already reaching for the coat hanging on the hook beside the front door. Her bag was in its usual place—ready on the wooden bench seat beneath it.

'They're no good,' the woman sobbed. 'They're only paramedics. He needs a doctor. He's—'

'Who is the patient and where do you live?' Kat demanded loudly, breaking into the woman's rising hysteria.

'Frank Leitner. At the off-licence. Hurry! Please, hurry! I've got him sitting against the wall and—'

'Phone for the emergency services!' Kat ordered sharply. 'Do it *now*!' And she put the phone down to thrust her second arm into her coat. Two paces took her to the kitchen doorway, a glimpse of Ben's frustrated expression telling her that he'd heard her half of the conversation and knew exactly what she was about to face.

'I feel so bloody useless!' he growled with a glare at his clumsy cast.

'You're not!' she countered. 'You're keeping an eye on my boys. And, anyway, as soon as that cast comes off, it'll be payback time, so don't get too comfortable. I'll be back as soon as I can.'

'Take all the time you need,' he said, not looking any more resigned to the situation. 'I'll be waiting here with my feet up.'

Kat was still grinning as she hurried out to the car, but the smile faded as she replayed the woman's words.

'She's got him sitting against the wall!' she repeated with a groan, a bad feeling growing when she totted up in her head exactly how long that might have taken. 'Why didn't the woman phone for the ambulance straight away? They could have been with her by now. As it is…'

She pulled up outside the front of the off-licence, making sure she left enough space for the ambulance when it arrived… '*If* the woman has made the call at all!' she muttered, as she grabbed her bag and hurried to the front door.

The bell rang over her head as she thrust it open, but she didn't even bother closing it when she saw the man facing her from the other end of the long aisle in front of her, his chin sunk all the way onto his chest.

'Mr Leitner?' she called, as she accelerated her pace towards him.

'I got him in the right position,' the woman on her knees beside him said proudly. 'They taught us how to do it at a first aid course about ten years ago, and I remembered!'

'Did you phone for the ambulance?' Kat demanded, as she joined her on the floor, depositing the bag beside her with a thud. One hand was already reaching out to lift the patient's head by supporting his forehead as the fingertips of the other probed the angle of his throat, hoping against hope to find the reassuring thump of a pulse in the man's carotid.

Nothing.

'I tried to find his pulse in his wrist, but I couldn't,' the woman said, relief at handing over responsibility for the man's health clear in her voice.

'Was he able to say anything to you?' Kat demanded, as she thumbed back first one eyelid and then the other. Fixed and dilated. Absolutely no response at all.

'Just that his chest hurt—and his arm—and that he couldn't breathe. He looked ever such a funny colour and—'

'And how long ago was that?' Kat interrupted the flow without a qualm as she flipped the catches on her bag and grabbed her stethoscope.

'About twenty minutes ago, but he hasn't said anything since I sat him like that… Oh, my word!' exclaimed the woman as Kat simply tugged the man's shirt wide open, sending buttons flying, knowing that there was no time for the niceties of undoing them. 'That's one of his best shirts! He won't be very happy about—'

'Shh!' Kat demanded curtly, as she pressed the stethoscope against the man's chest, and blessed silence fell. Unfortunately, it wasn't broken by the sound of a heartbeat or breathing. 'Damn!' she cursed, and sat back on her heels.

Was it worthwhile pounding on the man's chest just so it looked as if she was making an effort to resuscitate him, or should she simply tell the woman that positioning the man perfectly was all very well, but totally useless if he'd stopped breathing?

'Is he all right?' she demanded. 'I did everything right, didn't I?'

'You positioned him perfectly,' Kat said. 'Unfortunately, his heart stopped beating and he's not breathing so—'

'But you can get that going with one of those defibre-something machines, can't you?' she said cheerfully—*too* cheerfully? 'I've seen it on the telly. The patient's dead as mutton one minute, a quick zap and they're sitting up talking the next and…'

Kat shook her head slowly from side to side and the woman's words died away and her face crumpled. 'He's dead, isn't he?' she whispered, and reached a gentle hand out to stroke the pale grey face. 'I was afraid he was gone, but I had to do *something* to help him…'

Phoning for an ambulance straight away would at least have given him a ghost of a chance, Kat thought in frustration, but there was nothing she could do about it now. And there was no point in breaking the woman's heart by telling her she should have done anything differently.

The wailing sound of the ambulance hiccuped to a halt outside the shop and brought Kat to her feet.

'Come on, love,' she said gently, helping the older woman up from her knees. 'Let's go out and tell them what's happened. Perhaps we can get a paramedic to put the kettle on.'

'There's not a lot else he can do…not for Frank,' she said sadly. 'He always joked that he was the best boss I ever had…because he was the *only* boss I ever had.' Kat heard her gulp back tears. 'I came to work here straight from school and I've been here ever since. Employee…wife…partner…'

Widow, Kat finished for her, seeing the realisation dawn on the older woman's face and the tears start to fall. She could remember that moment only too well.

'Hi, Dr Leeman, we were told you needed—' The paramedic broke off with a grimace when she shook her head, her arm supportively around the sobbing woman's shoulders.

'Do you think you could find Mrs Leitner a cup of tea?' she suggested, and the burly man's face softened.

'No problem at all,' he said, as he gently took over the supporting role from Kat. 'You come with me, sweetheart. Show me where everything's kept.'

It was another hour before all the formalities were over and the body could be removed to the mortuary at the local hospital. The mere fact that it had been an unexpected death of someone who hadn't apparently had any previous heart problems meant that there would have to be a post-mortem.

But for now Kat's part in the proceedings was over and as soon as Pam Leitner's sister arrived to keep her company, she was free to go home.

And why did that thought immediately bring to mind a picture of a certain dark handsome man sitting in her lounge with his injured leg propped up on a footstool? Why, as she drove through the silent streets in the hour just before midnight, did her heart beat faster with the hope that Ben would be sitting up waiting for her to come home, when his time would be far better spent getting some sleep?

'Kat?' Ben's head poked around the door to her surgery when she'd answered his knock, the pile of paperwork in front of her seeming to have grown even taller than when she'd started on it.

'As soon as the practice can afford to employ someone to take over this unending form-filling, I'm advertising!' Kat growled, almost ready to tear her hair out. 'I'm supposed to be going to see Sam's first football match this afternoon— Oh!' She suddenly realised that Ben probably wasn't in her room to hear her moan. 'Was that what you wanted? Is it time to go?'

'No. There was a phone call from the school.'

Kat frowned and looked at the phone. Surely she hadn't ignored it when Rose had buzzed her to take the call?

'I was in the reception area and took the call while Rose was sorting out an appointment,' Ben explained. 'It was Sam's teacher to say he's been sick several times today and isn't feeling well.'

'Several times!' Kat exclaimed. 'Why didn't they phone me the *first* time? I'd have come to fetch him straight away.'

'That's why they didn't phone,' Ben said with a wry grin. 'Apparently, Sam begged them not to because otherwise he'd miss his football match.'

'And Sam can be very persuasive,' Kat conceded, dropping her pen on top of the paper equivalent of Mount

Everest in front of her and retrieving her handbag out of the locked drawer in her desk.

'Do you want me to get him?' Ben offered, and pointed to his foot with a bright grin. 'Remember, the smaller cast and an automatic car and I'm a member of the driving fraternity again! And I've already finished this afternoon's house calls. Or, better still, we could both go. Then, if it's just a false alarm, we can both see him play.'

'When you put it like that, it's difficult to turn you down, but hadn't we better take both cars, in case the phone rings?'

'Probably,' he conceded easily. 'Then, if you have to take Sam home early, I'll be on hand to collect Josh.'

Kat agreed with the logic of the plan even though she knew that Josh would be less pleased. Somehow, ever since Ben's long cast had come off a few days ago, her elder son had been growing increasingly antagonistic towards the man, in spite of the fact that Ben was just as willing to help him with his homework and give him sporting pointers when he practised his football in the back garden as in the preceding weeks. It was almost as though he suddenly saw the man as some sort of threat now that he was almost back to full strength.

But it wasn't Josh's internal struggles that consumed Kat as she hurried towards their school that afternoon, it was Sam.

Over the last few weeks it had been heartening to see the uncomplicated way her younger son had accepted Ben's presence in their lives…and the way he was returning to the bouncy, energy-filled child he'd always been. He'd had several rather nasty headaches since his fall in the bathroom but gradually the house had been filled with his infections giggles and abysmal jokes and she'd begun to breathe again to see his resilience restored.

There was no resilience visible in the miserably huddled child in the school's sick bay.

'Oh, Sam,' Kat whispered as she hurried to his side, having to skirt the strategically positioned bowl on the floor beside him. 'What's the matter, sweetheart?'

'Mum...my head,' he moaned miserably.

'Did you hit it in the playground? Did you get knocked over?' She began to run gentle fingers over the silky hair to look for any signs of bruising, but he gasped and feebly brushed her away, the movement of his hand visibly uncoordinated.

'D-don't...d-don't touch it...' he stammered, the words strangely slurred as though he was more than half-asleep. 'Hurts too much.'

An impossible thought came into her head...totally impossible because there was no way anything so dreadful could happen to her son... It just couldn't...

And then her eyes met Ben's over Sam's head and when she recognised in their depths the same expression of foreboding that filled her, her heart clenched in agony.

'He needs to go for tests as soon as possible,' Ben said softly, confirming aloud her own panicked thoughts.

No! screamed a voice inside her head but she silenced it instantly. This wasn't the time or the place to have hysterics, but she absolutely *couldn't* contemplate the fact that there might be something seriously wrong with her son, not so soon after losing Richard.

'Just to rule out anything...untoward,' she agreed shakily,

and when the shutters came down behind Ben's eyes blind terror took over.

He obviously thought it was something more. *He* knew that this wasn't just something minor that would go away without too much bother…

'Ben, I can't think…' she admitted, horrified to hear how her voice trembled. She needed to be strong, for Sam's sake. She cleared her throat, swallowed and drew a deep breath before she began again. 'I can't remember who to refer him to. Can you suggest someone? Someone *good*…the best!'

For just a moment his poker face failed him and she saw desolation in the depths of his eyes, then it was gone, back under control again.

'We need to get him to hospital first, to start some basic tests,' he pointed out calmly. 'That will give me some time to think…to contact some people…' He shook his head sharply. 'Of course it will depend exactly what's causing the problem…'

'Of course,' she agreed woodenly, as she scooped Sam into her arms. 'But when we know…if it's something…'

A stray corner of her brain registered the fact that her precious younger son seemed to have grown enormously recently and she wondered just how long it would be until she was no longer able to pick him up. Another grimmer corner wondered how many times she would have to cradle him if the cause of his problems was something…life-threatening…even malignant.

'I'll help you find someone,' Ben agreed in a voice that seemed to emerge through sharp-edged gravel. 'Someone good enough for Sam.'

The journey to the hospital was a nightmare for Kat, in spite of the fact that Ben had taken over all the arrangements.

He was the one who settled her in the back seat of his car so that she could take care of Sam on the journey. He had also arranged for the headmaster to fetch Josh and had got the number from Rose to arrange for emergency cover for the practice.

'I'm sorry if it gave you a fright, Josh, being called out of class like that,' she heard Ben apologise, as he started the engine and began the journey. 'But we're not sure how long we'll be at the hospital, and we didn't want you to be left waiting at school, not knowing what was going on.'

'So, what's wrong with Sam?' Josh demanded from his unaccustomed place in the front seat of a car, sounding closer to Sam's eight rather than his own eleven years of age, though he tried hard to sound grown-up. Kat's heart clenched anew, guessing that this was yet another burden he'd try to take on those slender shoulders. 'Is it something to do with when he fell in the bathroom?'

Before she could hasten to reassure Josh that it definitely *wasn't* his fault, Ben was speaking.

'It's possible that the same thing that caused him to fall in the bathroom is also causing him to be sick this time, too,' he agreed, far more calmly than *she* could ever have managed.

'But what *is* it?' Josh demanded. 'What's making him like this?'

Suddenly the slender body in Kat's arms grew rigid then began to thrash jerkily, his arms flailing with uncontrolled violence.

'Ben! He's fitting!' Kat gasped, as she tried to protect

Sam from hurting himself against the hard surfaces all around them without hurting him herself. 'Stop the car!'

'There's no point,' he said gruffly, the rising note of the engine witness to the speed at which they were now travelling in response to the new emergency. 'We haven't got anything in the car to help him and we're not far from the hospital. Can you hang on or do you want to swap places?'

'I wouldn't be able to drive,' she admitted bluntly, her teeth gritted against the need to howl out her terror. This wasn't her bright, beautiful boy writhing and jerking like this, this was… It was almost as if he'd been possessed by some malign spirit that had taken control of him…and with every fibre of her being, she wanted it gone.

Behind them there was the sudden blare of a police siren, just a warning burst of sound as the interior of Ben's car was lit by sharp stabs of bright blue light.

'No!' wailed Kat, unable to bear the thought of wasting a single second, explaining why they were going so fast.

'Josh, my bag's on the floor by your feet,' Ben said crisply, as the powerful car drew up beside them, the policeman in the passenger seat gesturing curtly for Ben to pull over to the side of the road. 'Flick the locks, take out the "Doctor on Call" card and hand it to me.'

Kat was too busy trying to protect Sam to see what was happening in the front of the car but she heard the approval in Ben's 'Good lad' and knew that Josh had done as he asked in a remarkably short time.

Then there was the roar of a powerful engine and the police car was pulling ahead of them with its sirens on full and Kat realised that the driver must have realised where they were going in such a hurry and had decided to clear their way.

'Oh, thank you, thank you,' she said under her breath, even though there was no way the officer could hear her.

'Oh, *wow*!' she heard Josh say fervently. 'We're going nearly *eighty* miles an hour!' And she almost managed a smile that he could find something so scary impressive. At least it proved that he was a normal boy underneath all the adult responsibilities he'd tried to assume since Richard's death.

Finally, just as Ben was pulling up in front of the entrance to the emergency department, Sam's fit came to a shuddering end.

The police must have patched some sort of warning through to the hospital because even as Ben was climbing out of the car, the hospital's automatic doors were opening and a team was hurrying a trolley towards them.

'Is Sam all right, Mum?' demanded Josh, as Ben lifted his brother's unconscious body from Kat's lap and deposited it gently on the trolley.

'I hope so, Josh,' she said, afraid to be any more positive than that. Josh knew only too clearly from a year ago that well-meaning everything-will-be-all-right promises were sometimes completely wrong. So that his trust wasn't shattered again, she refused to get his hopes up until she had some idea of the severity of Sam's condition. 'We won't know anything definite until they do some tests.'

Almost before Kat was out of the car and on her feet, the trolley had reversed direction and was being pushed back into the department at high speed, with Ben striding swiftly beside it. His deep, husky voice faded into the distance all too quickly as he recounted for the attending staff the details not only of this episode but also of the day Sam had fallen in the bathroom.

That fact alone was enough to bring home to her the potential seriousness of what was going on. That first incident had been several weeks ago, and apart from a cluster of headaches, Sam had seemed perfectly well ever since. Now Ben was linking the two together. Did that mean that whatever was causing it had been silently growing worse all that time?

'He's not going to…*die*, is he?' Josh whispered, his hand creeping into hers and hanging on tightly in a way he hadn't done for several years, as they hurried after the trolley into the emergency department.

What price honesty now? demanded a bitter little voice inside her head, but there was only one answer she could give her son, no matter how frightened he was.

'Josh…' She drew him out of the main stream of traffic and found a relatively quiet corner where she took both of his cold hands in hers and bent down to meet his gaze. A part of her was desperate to be with Sam, to know exactly what was happening to him and to protect him, but her first-born needed her too, and she could trust Ben to take care of her baby.

She could trust Ben…

That realisation was like the sun suddenly coming up over the horizon in the middle of the blackest of nights and gave her the courage to do what had to be done.

'Josh, I honestly don't know what's going to happen to Sam yet, because I don't know what's the matter with him,' she said, her voice thick with the tears she didn't dare to allow to fall. The first one would breach the dam and she might never be able to stop.

'Shouldn't we be with him?' Josh asked, his eyes flicking

from her face to the corridor down which his little brother had disappeared.

'That might be a problem because they don't usually let family members stay with the patient when they're…'

'Not even if they're doctors?' he demanded, clearly scandalised. 'What about Dr Ben? Will they make him come out, too? Will Sam be all on his own?'

Kat didn't think for a moment that Ben would leave Sam to the tender mercies of an unknown group of people, no matter how highly qualified. He would insist on knowing exactly what they were doing and why, and he would let her know as soon as—

'There he is!' exclaimed Josh, and set off at a run towards the man approaching down the corridor that angled past the reception desk and beyond.

'Dr Ben! Where's Sam? What's happened to him? Did they make you come out here to wait with the ordinary people?' Kat watched Josh come to an abrupt halt when the worst possibility of all hit him, his eyes enormous as he gazed up at Ben. 'Is he… Is Sam…*dead*?'

'Not at all, Josh,' Ben said immediately, wrapping a reassuring arm around Josh's shoulders before he looked up to meet Kat's eyes. 'In fact, he's woken up and is asking for his mum.'

For a moment Kat was filled with unutterable relief but then she saw the dark shadow behind Ben's smile and knew that he had bad news to tell her…news that he couldn't go into with Josh listening to their every word.

'Well, that definitely deserves a drink to celebrate,' Kat said brightly. 'Ben, have you got any change in your pockets for the machines over there? Perhaps Josh could get a couple of cans while you point out which room Sam is in, then the two of you can sit together till I come back out.'

Ben was quick on the uptake, suggesting not only a drink but giving Josh enough cash to choose a snack, too.

'Tell me,' she ordered, as soon as Josh was out of earshot, the haunted look on Ben's face terrifying her. 'How bad is it?'

'They're organising to take him up to Neuro-Radiology as soon as they can fit him in, hopefully today. If not, tomorrow.'

'Neuro-Radiology?' she repeated numbly, knowing exactly what that signified without needing to be told. 'What do you think it is? A bleed of some sort? A growth? Cancer?' The last word emerged as a whisper as she imagined the radio-opaque dye being injected into her son's circulatory system to outline whatever deadly *thing* was happening inside his head.

'Kat.' He took both her hands in his but their warmth and strength wasn't enough to thaw the terror that was freezing her heart. 'It's beginning to look very much as if it's a growth of some sort and…Kat, it's started pressing on the optic nerve.'

'The optic nerve?' Her brain was moving so sluggishly that it took her a moment to recognise the importance of those simple words. Then she understood and was horrified. 'Sam's going blind?'

CHAPTER SEVEN

'MUM? Why won't they let me have any lights on?'

Sam's plaintive question nearly broke her heart but she couldn't let him know it. Kat sent up a silent prayer of gratitude that Ben had warned her what had happened but it didn't lessen the shock of the reality.

His speech was growing more slurred, too. Was that just because of the drugs he'd been on since he'd been admitted, or because of whatever was going on inside his head?

'It's because of your headaches, sunshine,' she invented swiftly. 'They're hoping it will help them to go away until they can finish all their tests.'

'Does that mean I won't be able to watch any television?' he demanded, this time in horror. 'Or read my Harry Potter?'

'But, Sam, when your headache's bad, you don't like the noise of the television,' she began reasonably, abandoning that tack when she saw a mulish look curve the corners of his mouth downwards. 'Anyway, when it's not so bad, I could read Harry to you, couldn't I?'

He pondered the suggestion for a moment and she held her breath. He'd been so proud of the fact that he'd progressed enough to read the books by himself that she was worried that he might feel that she was treating him like a baby again, having to be read to.

'Would you do all the voices, like you did for the first books when Josh was learning to read?' he bargained, with a lightening of his expression.

'Is there any *other* way to read Harry Potter?' she teased, giving his hand a squeeze even as she desperately wanted to wrap him in her arms and protect him from the world. He looked so pale and it was frightening what strength of analgesia it was taking to dull the pain of his headaches. If she didn't find out soon what was causing this misery, she was going to…

'Dr Leeman?' called a soft voice from the doorway and she looked across to see the young registrar beckoning to her.

'I'll be back in a minute,' she promised Sam, daring to brush the lightest of kisses over his childishly smooth brow even as a huge lump of terror lodged under her heart. The young man hadn't had enough experience yet to keep his thoughts out of the expression on his face. She already knew that the news she was about to hear wasn't good.

'You try to have a sleep, sunshine, and when I come back, I'll read the next chapter to you,' she suggested, feeling as if her heart was breaking. She couldn't lose Sam, too. She just couldn't bear it. He was so precious…a perfect mixture of the best of both of his parents who deserved to have a long and happy life. Not…

'OK,' Sam agreed drowsily, gradually losing his fight against the latest dose of analgesia. 'See you in a minute…'

Kat found herself tiptoeing out of the room, although she knew that it would probably be several hours before the drugs wore off enough for the pain to rouse him again.

'The neuro-radiologist would like to have a word with you,' the young man announced, as though he was proclaiming an audience with some great deity. 'He's had the results of the tests.'

Kat barely heard his awe-filled chatter as she accompanied him to the great man's office, waiting politely while he knocked when her first instinct was to barge her way in and demand that the man do something to help her son.

The door was opened and the man himself invited her in.

'Jon Fox-Croft,' he introduced himself, with a gentle handshake that was completely at odds with the big bearded teddy-bear of a man that he was. He led her over to a small group of plain functional upholstered chairs and waited for her to sit before he folded himself into the one beside her.

'Dr Leeman…or may I call you Katriona?' he suggested in his soft-spoken way.

'Kat,' she corrected him, then realised that her terror and impatience had made her sound rather curt. 'I gave myself the nickname as soon as I learned to talk and refused to answer to anything else. My parents finally gave up trying to change my mind when I started school.'

'That's a shame. It's a beautiful name,' he said, with a smile that did nothing to ease her torment. Luckily, he was adept enough at reading people's faces to know that pleasantries weren't helping to relieve her tension. 'You'd rather I just got on with it?'

'Please,' she agreed fervently. 'I know from…' she gestured blankly towards the door and the young man who had brought her there, a man whose name she couldn't recall because it simply hadn't mattered. '…his face that the news isn't good. What have you found? Is it…cancer?'

'Honestly, we don't know yet,' he said firmly, and the straight way he met her eyes told her that he was telling the truth so far. 'Look, you're a doctor so this is a different situation to my usual patients. It will probably make more sense if I show you the scans and we take it from there.' He leapt up from the seat and strode across to flick the light on in the view box, then slotted the familiar multi-slice sheet of scans into position.

For some reason, the fact that these were the images of the inside of her son's head left her strangely light-headed with a buzzing noise in her ears.

'Whoa, Kat, take it easy,' he said, grabbing her elbow when her knees started to buckle. 'Do you want to sit down again for a minute?'

'N-no!' She deliberately drew in a deep breath and straightened her shoulders. 'I'll be all right. I just…'

'Perch yourself on the corner of the desk,' he suggested, sweeping the neat piles of paperwork cavalierly aside to make room for her. 'Can you see from there?'

Kat focused on the images with a murmured agreement, her eyes flicking rapidly from one to another in a frantic race to find…whatever it was that was threatening her child.

'Here it is,' he directed, pointing with a neatly manicured finger at one of the slices, outlining an alien mass inside her son's brain. 'And here is where it's started pressing on the optic nerves. Just the pressure of having something that size growing in his head is enough to give him the headaches, but it's the position that could have the greatest consequences for his sight. I don't need to tell you that it wouldn't take much for the optic nerves to be permanently damaged if we don't relieve the pressure on them.'

'So it *is* cancer?' she asked, as despair gripped her.

'I told you, Kat, we don't know, and we *won't* know unless or until we do a biopsy of some of the tissue. It could be benign.'

But he didn't think it was, Kat realised, picking up on the glimpse of sorrow that even a man as experienced as Jon Fox-Croft had been unable to betray, even though he'd avoided meeting her eyes.

'So when will you do the biopsy?' She had to force herself to live through this nightmare as though it were some horror film…one scene at a time…one frame at a time, if necessary.

'I've been in touch with a colleague of mine, a neurosurgeon.' He turned to face her directly again. 'He specialises in children's tumours. He's done some amazing things…brilliant things that few other people in the world would have attempted.'

'And…?' Hope rose in spite of her strict hold on herself. 'Where do I have to take Sam to see him? How long will we have to wait? What are the chances that he'll be able to do anything for Sam…that he'll even be willing to try?'

'He's already seen the scans,' he said, much to her surprise, then she realised that new technology meant such things could now be transmitted around the world in fractions of a second.

'What does he think?' she demanded eagerly. 'If there's anything he can do for Sam…anything at all…'

'We agreed that he needs to have an operation as soon as possible,' he said bluntly. 'It's essential to remove at least enough of…whatever it is to relieve Sam's headaches and to release the pressure on the optic nerves before the damage becomes permanent. At the least, that would give us some breathing room to decide on our plan of attack for the rest of it.'

'How soon would he know what he was dealing with, and when to do…?' Kat stopped, suddenly realising that she was beginning to babble. There were so many questions she needed answered and she just couldn't get the words straight in her head, let alone get them out of her mouth.

'The biopsy would be done while Sam was in the operating theatre,' the neuro-radiologist explained, taking pity on her agitation. 'The decision would be taken there and then how far to take the operation…how far it would be safe to remove the tumour. Eventually, he would aim to remove enough to stop it in its tracks without damaging too much of the surrounding structures and cause permanent disability, especially as his eyes are already involved. Then, if he discovers that it *is* malignant, we would have to look at the possibilities of chemotherapy and-or radiotherapy.'

'So what you're saying is that when I sign the consent form, I won't know how much or how little of an operation Sam will have until it's all over. That he might end up permanently blind or…' She visualised the other structures in that region of the brain and shuddered at the damage the operation could cause. But what choice was there when the tumour itself was already causing so much damage?

She was grateful that he was silent, apparently realising that she needed time to follow her train of thought uninterrupted.

In the end, it all came down to stark choices. Did she deny Sam an operation because she was afraid of the level of damage that could be done to his brain as the tumour was removed, or did she give the neurosurgeon permission to operate to avoid Sam's almost inevitable death?

'Do you trust him?' she demanded bluntly. 'If Sam were *your* child, would you trust this neurosurgeon to do the operation?'

Her respect for the man grew when he didn't rush into a glibly reassuring answer but took his time to consider her question.

'If my child's options were the same as Sam's, then, yes, I would go for the operation. Mr Rossiter hasn't been operating recently, but he's a phenomenal surgeon, brave and talented and, above all, caring. I *would* trust my child's life in his hands.'

Kat vaguely remembered the surgeon's name from something she'd read a while ago, probably in one of the journals that tended to pile up, largely unread for want of time. But, in the end, all medicine came down to trust. Her patients trusted her to do her best for them in diagnosing their ills and advising treatment accordingly. Jon Fox-Croft had been recommended by Ben when she'd needed the name of a neuroradiologist, and now she had a recommendation that this Mr Rossiter was the best person to perform Sam's operation.

'If I were to agree…how soon could he do the operation?' she asked, suddenly wishing that Ben could be there with her while she was making such monumental decisions. This was without a doubt one of the hardest things she'd had to do since she'd had to take up the reins as a single parent.

'As soon as possible,' he said grimly. 'These things are usually fairly slow-growing, the onset of symptoms so insidious that it's sometimes many months or even years before anyone thinks to start tests. In Sam's case…'

'It's only been a matter of weeks… at most, months,' Kat finished for him, terror building again with the thought that this might mean that it was more likely to be an aggressive malignant tumour…perhaps one that was already sending metastases throughout his body.

'Tell him…' She was breathing so fast that she was in danger of hyperventilating, terrified that she was making the wrong decision. Would Sam grow to resent her for putting him through hell just for the chance of a few more miserable months of life, or was the operation his one chance for a long and healthy future? 'Tell Mr Rossiter to do the operation as soon as he can.'

'Let me help you, Kat,' Ben said softly, when he saw the weary droop of her shoulders.

He reached out a hand to her then paused, startled to find that he actually *needed* to touch this valiant woman.

He'd only come down to the kitchen to retrieve the milk he'd left in her fridge, not wanting to disturb her in the night if sleep evaded him between call-outs. And there she was, sitting in the darkness in the kitchen, agonising about Sam and the fact that she'd had to leave him in hospital all by himself.

'You're already doing too much, Ben,' she objected. 'I'll be all right.' But the dark shadows under her eyes told a different story. If anything, they were worse than when he'd first met her, and that had been at the end of a year of trying to hold everything together virtually single-handed.

Sam's collapse had been the final straw, but she still couldn't bring herself to…what? Lean on him?

That was a laugh for a start. When had he ever welcomed anyone leaning on him? He'd never been there for even the people who'd meant most to him, so why should he expect someone he'd only known for a matter of weeks…someone he'd deliberately tried to keep at arm's length…to trust him enough to be there for her? Lorraine certainly hadn't been able to trust him to look after her, and as for Laura…

He shook his head, knowing to his cost that those were problems that he still had to come to terms with, situations that he dreamed about, wishing that he could wake up and find it had just been an ugly nightmare instead of his daily reality.

'And who's going to look after Josh and Sam when *you* collapse?' he demanded fiercely, trying to remember that Josh was sleeping just a little way down the hall. It had taken the poor kid ages to go to sleep that night, only finally succumbing after Ben had gone into his room and sat down with the offer of answering any questions.

'I can't ask Mum,' he'd explained, with eyes bright with the threat of tears. 'She's already so worried about Sam that I don't want her to have to think about me, too.'

So Ben had explained the tests that Sam had undergone since he'd been admitted to hospital and had shown him in one of Richard's textbooks exactly where the optic nerves were. He'd tried to put his mind at ease about the operation that would be performed, but had quickly realised that those details were a step too far.

Finally, it had been the promise that he would explain everything that happened over the next days and weeks that had allowed Josh to give in to his exhaustion.

If only he could get Kat to do the same.

'Please, Kat, be sensible.' He gave in to temptation and lowered his hands onto her shoulders, not surprised to feel her muscles knotted with tension. Slowly he rotated his thumbs, gently beginning to work on them in the hope that he could un-knot them. Otherwise she wasn't going to be able to go to sleep even if she did go to bed.

'You need to get a locum in,' he continued, trying to keep his mind off the feel of her slender bones under his fingers and the way the fine fabric of her shirt slithered over her skin. 'We need someone extra to cover the on-call hours, at least until you know Sam's going to be all right.'

'But the cost…' she began, and he tightened his grip just enough to give her a tiny shake.

'Kat, what does the cost matter if it gives you the time to be there for your boys? They've already lost so much…you *all* have. Don't make this harder on any of you than it has to be.'

'But…' This time he just gave her a warning squeeze, so very conscious of the fragility of the slender shoulders cupped in his palms. She gave the impression of being so strong—that she was effortlessly holding everything together—but then he came across her like this, looking utterly beaten, and he just wanted to wrap her in his arms and…

No! the warning voice in his head shouted. *Never again!* He'd been through that particular hell once and it had nearly destroyed him…it *had* destroyed something important inside him that had never recovered.

Anyway, this wasn't about him. This was about Kat and her two boys…Josh, oh so serious Josh, who was struggling so hard to be the man of the house at eleven years of age and Sam, bouncy, loving, loveable Sam, whose whole life was hanging in the balance waiting for that terrifying surgery to tip the balance one way or the other…

'Be logical, Kat,' he said gently, deliberately blanking out the thoughts of the upcoming surgery. That was something he didn't want to think about until the last possible moment. 'Sam needs you to spend time with him every bit as much as you want to be with him, but Josh needs you, too. If you were a stay-at-home mum it would be hard enough sharing yourself out between them, but with the practice to run and patients depending on you, too… You're not Superwoman, you know. And if you collapse, it might be at the very moment that the boys need you most.'

This time when her shoulders slumped under his ministering thumbs he knew he'd made his point and he released a sigh of relief even as she softly murmured her agreement.

'We can work a visiting rota out between us,' he suggested. 'And Rose has offered to stay on to keep Josh company at the end of surgery to give you extra time at the hospital. Then there's Josh's friends, too.'

'Josh's friends?' Her voice sounded husky with exhaustion but she was still following every word.

'He was telling me this evening that several of them—his closest mates—have offered to have him over to stay while Sam's in hospital.'

'Oh, but—'

'Apparently, he told them very politely that he was grateful for the offer, but he didn't really know how long Sam was going to be in, and could he let them know later.' He felt her chuckling through his fingertips and was glad she'd managed to find some humour in the situation.

'To be honest, I feel a bit like a gerbil in an exercise wheel—running my little legs off and getting nowhere,' she admitted, then twisted under his hands to look up at him over her shoulder. 'Thank you for making me stop and think what

I'm doing,' she said, those soft grey eyes of hers more peaceful than he'd seen them in several days. 'Of course, you're right about needing someone to take up the slack. I was probably ducking it because it's so difficult trying to get anyone worth having…someone who will take some of the load *off* my shoulders rather than putting more on.'

'You mean, someone of my calibre?' he teased when all he wanted to do was bend down and taste those pale pink lips. They weren't particularly lush and he doubted they'd seen any lipstick since first thing that morning—if then—but with a suddenness that nearly took his breath away, the desire to see what they felt like against his was overwhelming.

Then the guilt hit him with the force of a giant wrecking ball.

Could he really be getting over Lorraine so easily, so quickly? Did it really take nothing more than a pair of soft grey eyes and a grateful smile to dull the edges of bitter loss and make remorse fade into a soft-edged memory? He'd been so certain that he'd never recover from the events of that disastrous time that he'd completely changed his whole life. Had it all been a waste of time if he could forget so soon?

'So,' he said, playing for time and trying to remember what stage their conversation had reached before his emotions had gone haywire.

Ben withdrew his hands from her shoulders with more haste than subtlety and stepped away to begin pacing from one side of the room to the other. Perhaps a little distance would get his blood flowing in the right direction again.

'If you make out a list of times that you want to be at the hospital with Sam, and fill in the times you want to spend with Josh, we'll take that as the skeleton of a timetable,' he suggested. 'Then, once I've marked off any times I need off, we'll know what sort of cover we'll need the locum to do. OK?'

'I suppose so, but it seems like the wrong way to run a practice,' she said, clearly worried. 'What sort of effect will that have on continuity of care for the patients?'

'If you don't mind, I was thinking of putting up a small notice in the waiting room,' he suggested. 'I thought that if we explained that Sam's in hospital and that your hours are going to be shorter for the next few weeks, the patients would be more understanding if things weren't quite as...'

'Smooth-running as usual?' she offered with a wry smile, then nodded. 'That would mean that anyone who didn't really mind who they saw as long as they had an appointment with a doctor could take pot luck with whoever was available.'

'And those who particularly wanted to see you would have the option of waiting a little longer until you had an appointment free,' he finished. 'Exactly. What do you think?'

She was silent for so long, those grey eyes so serious and intent as she gazed up at him, that he started to feel the rising heat of a blush before she finally spoke.

'What I think is that I'll never be able to thank you enough for applying for this job,' she said fervently. 'I honestly don't know what I would have done without you.'

Ben looked so...*haunted* these days, Kat thought as she sat quietly beside Sam's bed, waiting for him to wake up. Several times she'd caught him staring into the distance and she had the impression that black thoughts were casting shadows in his eyes, darkening their colour to deep forest green.

And yet he certainly wasn't so introspective that he didn't notice when her own fears began to get the better of her.

The last couple of days, he seemed to have spent every spare moment either with Sam or with Josh, keeping their spirits up and the shared load had certainly made her life easier. Then there was the time that he spent with her in the evening, mostly just keeping her company and trying to persuade her to look forward to a positive outcome.

Fortunately—or was it unfortunately?—he hadn't picked up on the fact that what she most wanted was a hug. She wasn't looking for anything sexual…although now she thought about it, that would be a wonderful way of working off some of the tension that had built up inside her, and would work beautifully as a sleeping pill, but a hug of comfort would be… Oh, just the thought of it made her eyes burn with the threat of tears.

How long had it been since someone had hugged her? Not a childish hug. Sam was still free with those, although Josh was getting more circumspect about where they were before he'd indulge, but what she wanted…needed…was a hug from an adult male that was evidence that he genuinely cared about her.

'Some hopes!' she scoffed softly, and saw Sam's hand twitch in response to the sound. 'Are you awake, sunshine?' she asked softly, and felt her smile wobble when he whimpered in reply, the tape keeping his eyes closed for protection preventing him from seeing who was there unless they spoke.

'Mum…my head…!' he moaned, his little hand coming up to hover over it as if even he couldn't bear to touch it in case it made the pain worse.

A quick glance at the time told her that enough time had elapsed since his last dose of analgesia to permit another, even as the automatic pump clicked into action. Her concern that there was so little pain-free time between one dose and the next told her that the pressure inside his head must be rising. Her terror grew with that realisation. Was the tumour growing faster and if so, what were the chances that it would be benign? As far as she'd been able to ascertain, the benign tumours were relatively slow-growing but, then, she hadn't been able to make herself do any exhaustive research. The little she'd seen on her first Internet search had been terrifying enough.

'How long till the operation?' Sam asked, his tone coming so close to begging that her heart clenched with pity. It wasn't fair that her precious son was going through this…it wasn't fair that *any* child had to go through it, but Sam had already been through his share of misery in the last year. Wasn't losing his father enough for him to bear?

'In the morning, sunshine,' she reminded him, knowing that the analgesia was making his time perception faulty. 'You'll be the first one to go down to Theatre and Josh and I will be here, waiting for you to come back up.'

'He can listen to Harry while he's waiting,' Sam offered, but it took Kat several seconds to understand what he'd said, his speech was so slurred.

'Listen to Harry?' she repeated, not certain she'd heard right. Sam knew that Josh hadn't needed anyone to read to him for years now.

'Ben brought Harry…so I could listen…when no one's here…' he stumbled, one hand waving vaguely in the direction of the bedside cabinet.

Kat reached out and picked up the box from the top of the cabinet and realised it contained the audio version of the Harry Potter book she'd been reading to him. 'Is it good?' she managed, touched by Ben's thoughtfulness. With the best will in the world, she couldn't be here every minute that Sam was awake. Who would have thought that such a clever idea would have occurred to a man without children...?

'It's not as good as you,' he finished loyally, as his voice slid inexorably towards sleep again. 'I like your voices best.'

'Hey, Josh! You're here!' Sam said the next morning as he lay waiting for the trip to Theatre, unashamedly returning his big brother's gentle hug.

Kat couldn't help noticing that his body looked skinnier than ever against the pile of pillows, the oversized cotton gown with the faded cartoon characters on it bringing home exactly how young he was to be going through something as earth-shattering as this.

'Ben said he'd have a word with them, so I could be here in Dad's place,' Josh explained with quiet pride. 'But they made us all scrub our hands with some horrid stuff so we didn't bring any germs in to you.'

Kat had been so pleased to find that cleanliness and hygiene was paramount around Sam. His surgeon had apparently insisted upon it, pointing out that an infection by something like MRSA through an incision into his brain was unthinkable.

'Is Ben here?' Sam demanded, with a brief flash of eagerness that told Kat just how much her younger son admired the man...probably loved him, too, knowing the youngster's generous heart.

'He said to tell you that he'd definitely be here to have a word with you before you go into Theatre,' Josh reported, his earlier wariness of the man apparently a thing of the past as he faithfully delivered Ben's message.

'Good,' Sam said with a slightly wobbly smile, already more asleep than awake thanks to the pre-med. 'I wanted to thank him…for bringing me Harry to listen to.'

'Knock, knock,' said a voice at the door, and Kat was surprised to see Jon Fox-Croft's bearded face appear. 'Is this the lair of the Leeman? The Sam Leeman who's waiting for a ride?'

'That's me,' Sam said, his chin wobbling with his first display of nerves. 'Mum?' His voice wavered and held his hand out to her, blindly searching to make sure she was still beside him.

'I'm here, Sam,' she reassured him. 'I'll come with you all the way to the last door before they send you off to sleep.'

'Mum, I'm scared,' he whispered, unable to see the circle of staff surrounding him to prepare him for the journey to Theatre, or the fact that his words affected every one of them.

Kat certainly wasn't immune. It took every bit of strength she had not to start crying there and then, wishing with everything in her that she could undergo this in her son's place.

'OK, I think we're ready to roll,' the big gentle bear of a man announced, before turning to Josh. 'Young man, I'm giving you an important task. I'm putting the precious Harry Potter in your hands for safe-keeping until our return. Guard it with your life.' He leaned forward and added in an aside, 'And if you want to listen to it while you're waiting, that's one of the perks of the job.' Then he straightened up to his full impressive height again. 'So, Sir Joshua, do you accept your task?'

'Yes, sir. I accept,' Josh said seriously, then immediately sat on the nearest chair to open the box and sort through the discs with a grin on his face.

'I'll see you in a few minutes, Josh,' Kat said, grateful that the neuro-radiologist's ploy had distracted him from the tension of the moment as she kept pace with Sam's bed, his little hand clutching hers fiercely.

CHAPTER EIGHT

'HELLO, Sam. I promised I'd be here to speak to you before you had your operation,' Kat heard Ben say on the other side of the door that had just closed behind her, and her heart gave an extra leap.

Sam had been fretting all the way up to Theatre that Ben wouldn't know where to find him, and as much as she'd worried that something would prevent Ben fulfilling his promise, it was such a relief to know that he'd been utterly trustworthy.

A crazy part of her wanted to wait for him so that they could walk back to Sam's room together, but Josh was waiting for her, and her duty as a mother had to come before her sudden longing for the man's company.

Anyway, it wasn't as if he could stay with Sam for very long, with the eminent neurosurgeon waiting for him to be taken into theatre to start the operation. Knowing that Ben had booked himself out of the practice, too, she knew that he would be joining them soon to help Josh pass the time till his brother was out of the operating theatre.

Except Ben didn't join them until the operation was over and Jon Fox-Croft had been delegated to come up to tell them that all had gone well.

Kat was disappointed not to have the chance to thank Mr Rossiter personally, but logic told her that he must be a very busy man, with operating time at a premium. Perhaps she would have her chance to express her appreciation for what he'd tried to do for Sam when it was time for his post-operative check-up.

But that was in the future. The present was the sight of Ben coming into Sam's room looking like death barely warmed up.

'Ben! What's happened?' Kat demanded, her disappointment that he hadn't kept Josh and her company through the nerve-racking wait suddenly swamped by a fear so awful that it was almost impossible to find the words. 'Is it…Sam? Jon's only just been up to tell us that everything went well. Has something happened? Did something go wrong?'

'No, Kat, no,' he soothed, dredging up a smile that was so strained it didn't do much to ease her mind. 'We've…they've just had confirmation from the lab that the tumour *was* benign, and the margins were fairly clearly defined, so it was easier to work out what was tumour and what was brain tissue. Anyway,' he hurried on as though recognising that she wanted to query why he'd been told so many details before she had, 'I just came to tell you that they've now got him settled in ICU so you can visit him for a few minutes—just to put your mind at rest. Unfortunately, even my persuasive powers aren't enough to get Josh in for a visit yet, so we men will keep each other company till you get back.'

Kat's relief that the death sentence of a malignancy had been finally removed was so profound that it took an act of will to stop her knees buckling.

'But…' She'd anticipated that Josh wouldn't be allowed

to go into ICU—at least, not immediately post-operatively—and had prepared him for it. And she *was* grateful that Ben was willing to wait with him, especially as she had a feeling that her son was going to pepper Ben with myriad questions that he didn't want to ask *her* in case he upset her, but still…that didn't stop her wanting Ben to come with her, to be with her the first time she saw her precious little boy connected to all those monitors, when she'd be completely helpless to do anything for him.

'It all went well, Kat,' he reassured her quietly, when she still hovered uncertainly in the doorway, and he sounded so absolutely certain that it released her from her temporary paralysis.

'I'll be back soon,' she said, and was halfway along the corridor before she realised that she'd directed the words at Ben rather than Josh.

It was several hours before Kat felt confident enough about Sam's recovery that she'd allow Ben to persuade her to go home for the night.

Even then, with Josh finally sleeping the sleep of the emotionally exhausted and nothing left to scrub or tidy, she was so tense with residual adrenaline that she couldn't sit down for more than a minute, let alone contemplate sleep.

'Hey! If you need something else to clean and tidy, you can come upstairs and start on mine,' Ben teased quietly from the doorway.

She was so pleased to see him leaning negligently against the doorframe that it took a moment to register how drained and fatigued he looked, and guilt struck hard.

'Oh, Ben, I'm so sorry!' she exclaimed softly, as always

aware of her sleeping son. 'Am I keeping you awake, rattling around down here?'

'No. It's nothing like that,' he said dismissively, then paused for a moment before adding, 'Actually, I can't sleep either. My brain just doesn't want to shut down.'

She took a couple of steps closer and only then realised that it was something more than exhaustion he was suffering from.

'Ben…?' The only trouble was, she had no idea if anything was worrying him—she knew so little about him. In all the weeks that he'd been there, he seemed to have deliberately avoided talking about himself so she didn't know where to start.

Then he looked at her…*really* looked at her…and the emptiness and desolation she saw inside him were enough to break her heart.

'Will you come upstairs a minute, Kat?' he asked suddenly, seeming to come to a decision about something.

She almost made a comment about inviting her up to do his cleaning but realised that a joke would be out of place. His invitation had a far more serious purpose.

The upstairs room felt different somehow since he'd moved in, not part of her home any more but Ben's domain with a pair of well-worn jeans draped over the back of the chair, an untidy pile of books and an open laptop computer on the desk in the corner, with the screen showing the same Internet research site she'd accessed when Sam had first been diagnosed. There was a single coffee-cup left upside down to drain by the tiny sink but the less than perfectly made bed dominated everything.

Not that she would allow herself to look in that direction

again once she'd realised that just the thought of Ben lying on that bed was enough to raise her pulse rate. Anyway, he was striding in the other direction, towards the plain, functional desk and something hidden behind the pile of books.

For a moment he held whatever it was cradled in his hands before he turned and took the few steps to bring him back to her.

'This is…*was* Lorraine,' he corrected himself as he held out a framed photo towards her with a visibly trembling hand.

Kat took it from him and felt a vicious twist of jealousy when she saw the beautiful slender woman laughing up at a younger, infinitely happier Ben, who returned her gaze with adoration in his eyes, his mouth softened by the sort of smile she'd never seen on him—the sort of smile that said he loved her enough to move mountains for her.

'She was my wife, until she died of a brain tumour… glioblastoma multiforme,' he announced harshly.

'Oh, Ben!' she breathed, suddenly understanding why he'd seemed so distant that day. It must have been so hard for him to find out that Sam had a brain tumour, too. No wonder he hadn't been able to face waiting with her during the surgery. Just the fact that he'd been able to force himself to be there to fulfil his promise to Sam was more than enough.

'It's my fault that she died,' he said starkly, and any sympathetic platitudes she might have uttered were strangled in her throat.

'I don't believe it, Ben,' she said with utter certainty, not a single doubt in her mind. She couldn't imagine this caring man ever being the cause of a patient dying, let alone his wife. 'Tell me how…why…'

'She died because I was so damned busy with my patients that I didn't even notice what was happening right under my nose—at least, not until it was too late to do anything,' he said in a voice laden with self-condemnation, and with a flash of certainty she knew that he probably hadn't spoken to many—if any—about this. Probably, like her, he'd made certain that he was just too busy to even think about it rather than deal with the suffocating press of emotional overload.

The onset of Richard's illness had been so insidious, its progression so sudden and his decline so catastrophic that she hadn't even told her parents he was sick by the time she'd realised that he wasn't going to survive.

They'd been with her for the funeral, of course, but she'd put up such a good front, built on a foundation of grief and guilt, that they'd honestly believed her when she'd told them it was all right for them to return to Cyprus. And since then…

Since then, she'd barely had time to breathe, let alone grieve for Richard and come to terms with her guilt that she hadn't noticed her husband was ill.

The fact that Sam, her precious, laughing, mischievous boy, was lying in an ICU bed at this very minute was just one more unbearable…

'She had headaches—I suggested she take a painkiller,' Ben began again in a voice hollow with self-condemnation.

Kat waited silently for the rest of the story, her heart going out to him as the sentences came out one by one, jerky… staccato. She knew that feeling, as if everything inside was frozen and had to be hacked off a chunk at a time.

'She felt giddy—I blamed her latest diet,' he continued, 'She was always on a diet, even though she didn't need to lose an ounce.' He shook his head with a reminiscent smile and Kat could tell that he was remembering those days as clearly as she could remember teasing Richard about his habit of leaving the post in a welter of flyers from drugs companies, empty envelopes and important business matters, the resulting heap needing hours longer to sort out and file than if they'd been dealt with as they'd been opened. It had been an individual quirk of his character that she'd missed dreadfully when he hadn't been there any more.

'Then, completely out of the blue, she collapsed and before I even got to her side…before they could get hold of me, she went into a coma, and I never…I never even got to say…'

Suddenly, without any warning, this strong man was reaching out to her, with the first tears streaming down his ashen cheeks and the first sob ripping its way out of his throat.

What else could she do other than wrap her arms around him and draw him across to sit on the side of the bed?

Even as she was contemplating the enormity of Ben's loss, she was thinking how easily that could have been Sam's diagnosis, too. In fact, the speed with which his symptoms had developed had made it almost a foregone conclusion that they would be dealing with one of the more aggressive malignancies. To be told that the tumour had been benign had been like winning the top prize in the greatest lottery of all…life.

Suddenly, the fact that this strong man was sobbing his grief out in her arms allowed her to release her tight control on her own emotions and she began to weep, too…with relief that Sam's prognosis was so much better than she could ever have imagined, mixed with long-delayed sorrow for the husband she'd never had time to mourn, and added to that was sympathy for the curtailed life of the woman Ben had lost.

'I'm sorry,' he groaned, as he buried his face deeper into the curve of her neck, his arms tightening inexorably around her. 'I shouldn't be—'

'Shh!' she soothed, feeling a strange sense of catharsis that they could actually share this almost primitive experience. She drew in a shuddering breath. 'You've got nothing to be sorry for,' she insisted, for some reason feeling as protective of him as she was of her two boys.

'But I should have…*seen*,' he argued brokenly. 'I should have *known* that there was…something wrong.'

'It wouldn't have made any difference,' she pointed out stubbornly, tightening her hold on his head and pressing her cheek tightly against his so that their tears mingled freely. 'You know as well as I do what an evil thing glioblastoma multiforme is. You know that even if you'd spotted it earlier, in time for her to go through everything—operations, chemo, radiotherapy—none of it would have done anything except delay the inevitable.' The fact that *that* was the exact scenario she had envisioned for Sam made their conversation even more poignant.

'But…' He shook his head, ready to argue further, but she tightened her grip, sliding her fingers through the thick dark hair at the nape of his neck, and when she tugged gently to raise his head to force him to meet her gaze she caught a glimpse of the stray silver strands at his temples.

There was a heavy shadow of his emerging beard over his jaw and under the hospital scent of the alcohol-based hand cleanser they'd all had to use, she could smell the unique mixture of soap and pheromones that was Ben.

'Immersing yourself in remorse doesn't work, Ben,' she said softly, earnestly, believing it was the truth. 'I tried it with Richard…blaming myself that I didn't spot his illness sooner…telling myself that he wouldn't have suffered— wouldn't have *died*—if only I'd taken more notice. But there's only so long that you can live with survivor's guilt before it starts to eat at you from the inside…especially when simple logic tells you that there is absolutely nothing you can do to change what's already happened.'

Something she was saying must have penetrated the miasma of misery that surrounded him because he was actually focusing on her now. The tears were still welling out of reddened eyes and sliding inexorably down, but he was obviously taking in what she was saying, knowing that she was speaking from experience, having gone through exactly the same trauma a little over a year ago.

He was silent for a long time and she could almost hear the gears turning as he processed what she'd said.

'Ah, Kat,' he said on a shaky sigh, and when he pressed his forehead against hers, she felt all the corrosive tension drain out of him. 'Why couldn't I have met you sooner?' he asked, as he tilted his head to brush the lightest of kisses on the corner of her startled lips.

Her eyes widened at the sudden electricity that arced between them at the contact and she stared at him, close enough to see the endearing way his tears had made spiky clumps of those thick dark lashes and the way his pupils were dilating even as she watched.

Did she look as startled as she felt? Did she wear the same

expression on her face as he did, a combination of shock, questioning and a sudden overwhelming need?

Whatever he saw in her eyes, it definitely prompted him to do it again, his lips surprisingly soft and gentle as they stroked over hers, lingering just long enough for her to recognise desire kindling inside her.

The third time their lips met was a revelation.

It wasn't the kind of kiss she was used to—Richard's kiss—tender, loving, considerate. Instead, it was hot and hard and desperate, as though he was a man dying of thirst and she was his only source of water… And suddenly she was every bit as desperate.

And then kissing wasn't enough for either of them.

With an abandon that she'd never known before, Kat found herself struggling with buttons and zips, her hands tangling with Ben's as they alternately tugged at each other's clothing and then their own.

She had never felt like this before, not even in the early heady days after she and Richard had married, as if…as if she would fly apart into a million pieces if she couldn't have him—all of him—right this second.

There was a brief moment…when she stood in front of him with nothing but the soft golden brightness of the bedside light gilding her skin…when she suddenly remembered that her body showed the evidence of two pregnancies and she froze like a rabbit caught in a car's headlights.

But then his hands reached for her, oh, so eagerly, and she forgot everything but the feeling of his powerful body pressed tightly against her. And then his hands, his beautiful, strong, talented hands, stroked her all over as though he could never tire of touching her, exploring her, pleasuring her. Then even that wasn't enough and she knew the sensation of his arms wrapping around her, lifting her off her feet as though she weighed no more than a feather, positioning her and joining with her as they were caught up in a vortex of delight that left them both panting and exhausted.

It was still dark when Kat's common sense reasserted itself several hours later.

She felt utterly boneless with satisfaction, her head sharing the only pillow left on the bed when they'd finally dragged the quilt up off the floor to cover themselves.

The soft light was still burning beside the bed, and even though she knew that she should be gathering up her clothes to go down to her own room, she allowed herself just a moment or two to gaze at Ben while he slept.

His face was very different in sleep, younger-looking, with the hint of a smile curving the corners of his mouth. Was he having a pleasant dream? About them? She wished that she had the nerve to wake Ben and ask him. Then, she knew, she wouldn't have to do much to entice him into one last kiss, and he would be bound to pull her down onto the bed and...

She was shaking her head at the foolishness of her thoughts when his expression flattened out and then drew into the beginning of a frown, and she realised anew just how little she knew about this self-contained man.

Even as she was making her way down the spiral staircase, barefoot on the wrought-iron treads so she didn't risk waking either of the men in the silent household, in her head she was trying to gather together the things she *did* know about him.

First and foremost, he was a caring man and an exceptional GP and ever since he'd met them he'd been endlessly patient with her two boys, in spite of the fact that Sam had precipitated his broken leg. Even when Sam had been pestering him for attention and Josh had been throwing him resentful looks for intruding on his father's territory, he'd responded like a man totally at home with the vagaries of children.

'And then there's the obvious!' she muttered softly in the dark emptiness of her bedroom as she groped for the nightdress folded under her pillow. She certainly hadn't needed long-sleeved brushed cotton to keep her warm, with his body arousing her to fever pitch. 'Oh, yes, the man knows how to make love,' she whispered softly into the pillow, her cheeks flaming at the memories of the second time, when they'd finally made it to the bed and Ben had given her free rein with his body.

Then she felt a flash of guilt when she realised that Richard's love-making had never caused her to feel like this, even though she'd loved him enough to marry him and bear his children. Did Ben feel this way about Lorraine…guilty for experiencing such pleasure with someone new?

But they had been so good together *before* they'd discovered their compatibility in the bedroom, with every day that they worked together proving how alike their approach was to the practice of family medicine.

Even in their off-duty hours, when he'd joined the three of them to share a meal or played football with the boys or even something as simple as the way he seemed to automatically pick up a cloth to begin drying while she was washing up.

She'd never had another person so much in tune with her thoughts and feelings and didn't know why it should be happening with Ben, especially as he'd been so reticent about letting her get to know him. Did the feeling of 'connection' stem from some strange sort of subconscious kinship between the two of them…the result of the fact that both of them had lost a loved one?

One thing she didn't understand was why he hadn't said something about his wife's death sooner. Obviously it wasn't the sort of topic he would want to bring up at a job interview, but over the weeks since then she had spoken of Richard several times, as had the boys. Surely, at some stage he could have said…something.

Then she remembered the strange 'closed-in' expression on his face when he'd come for the interview and realised with a flash of intuition that he had done exactly that when Lorraine had died—he'd closed in on himself and kept all the grief locked up inside him.

So what had changed? What had last night been about?

'Was it the first crack in the wall?' she whispered, as her heart gave a foolish leap of hope. Had it been the first step as he began the long process of healing, or had it been something more? Could it be that his feelings towards her were growing as fast as hers, that they might be falling…

'Don't go there,' she warned herself, suddenly terrified that she was letting her imagination run riot. In all the weeks that he'd been there, he'd never so much as hinted that he saw her as anything other than a professional colleague with whom she also had a relaxed friendly relationship in out-of-duty hours.

Had the emotional meltdown made them vulnerable enough that a single kiss had caused such a conflagration? Would he be full of regrets in the morning for his uncharacteristic loss of control or would it be the start of a new chapter…the beginning of a deeper relationship that could eventually lead to…?

'Enough! Go to sleep' she ordered herself, knowing that any more speculation was futile. She knew that her feelings were already far deeper than she'd realised, her heart already trembling on the brink of for ever, but in spite of the intimate hours they'd spent together in his bed, she honestly had no idea if Ben felt the same.

'I'll know when I see him in the morning,' she whispered, with a shiver that combined excitement with dread. She'd never had to deal with a 'morning-after' situation before, so had no idea what she should say or how she should behave towards him.

Was it correct etiquette to walk up to him for a kiss? Would he welcome such daring? She had absolutely no idea. But she would know how he felt about what had happened as soon as she saw the expression in his eyes. He might put on a poker face but after last night she'd realised that she only had to watch his eyes and she would know.

'Oh, for heaven's sake!' she grumbled aloud, totally unable to switch her brain off. There were so many things she had to do in the morning, before she could be where she wanted to be…at Sam's bedside.

The combination of mannitol and corticosteroids seemed to be controlling the swelling in Sam's brain, caused by the trauma of the surgery, and if he'd had a good night, the consultant was hoping to lessen the cocktail of drugs that were keeping him so heavily sedated. It would be a while before they knew whether the tumour would grow again, but it was only when the drugs were withdrawn and he was allowed to wake up that they would know exactly how much damage had been done to his brain in its removal.

The familiar sound of a door closing had her sitting bolt upright in the bed while she strained her ears for some other sound to tell her who was up and about at this hour of the morning. Had Josh been unable to sleep or…?

The sound of Ben's car starting seemed abnormally loud in the darkness and had her out of bed and sprinting towards the window to catch just a fleeting glimpse of taillights as he disappeared out of the driveway.

'Where has he gone?' she demanded with a sudden sense of dread, knowing it wasn't a visit to a patient because they'd arranged for the covering service to take their calls while Sam was in hospital. Anyway, she had one of the phones on her bedside cabinet and it definitely hadn't rung. But where else would he be going at this time of night…unless…?

Fear that she knew exactly what he was doing had her running silently along the hall and back up the stairs again, her need for silence almost swamped by her need to know whether Ben had just driven out of her life, unable to face her in the morning.

The sight of the wreckage they'd made of his bed was enough to bring a blush to her cheeks but she forced her eyes away to look around the room.

'It's still here,' she breathed, as relief turned her knees to water and she sank to the floor. 'Everything's still here,' she said, as she catalogued the presence of his books and clothes, his computer and especially the photo of his wife. She knew he would never leave without Lorraine's photo.

So, where had he gone, and why?

Had he been unable to sleep, too? Had he done nothing

more than go out for a drive so he didn't disturb the two of them sleeping downstairs?

'Wherever he's gone, it's none of my business,' she muttered firmly, as she peeled herself up off the floor and retraced her steps down the spiral staircase. 'I must get some sleep if I'm going to be able to cope with the day ahead.'

That was especially true if Sam was going to be weaned off his drugs today. She was going to need all her strength while she waited to see if he was still her bubbly, irrepressible Sam or if the life-saving surgery had caused irreversible damage to his personality.

'What on earth have I done? What was I thinking?' Ben demanded softly of the bleeping machines that monitored Sam's every breath and heartbeat.

He groaned as he leaned forward, planting his elbows on his knees and cradling his head between his hands, and stifled a snort of disgust. That was the problem in a nutshell. He *hadn't* been thinking. He'd allowed his emotions to get out of control and the next thing he'd known he'd been sitting there blubbering all over Kat's shoulder like a baby.

And after that? Well, there was no excuse for the way he'd betrayed Lorraine's memory like that, even though Kat—sweet, generous Kat—had seemed to welcome every minute of their intimacy.

The guilt of sharing his bed with her was overwhelming, but even so he was honest enough to admit that no other woman had ever had that trigger-quick effect on him. Not even Lorraine.

All Kat had needed to do had been to stir against him in her sleep and he'd been desperate for her all over again. In fact, he'd lost count of the number of times he'd turned to her but each time she'd opened her arms to him and…

One of the monitors gave an extra bleep, automatically jerking his eyes up to check that all was still well, but that was enough to break his train of thought.

He cast a professional eye over the youngster even while he castigated himself for allowing his thoughts to wander like that. It hardly seemed appropriate to be thinking that way about his mother while Sam was lying in a drugs-induced coma right in front of him. But if his choice was between sitting here with Sam and fighting his explicit memories or going back to Kat's house and try to stop himself begging to be allowed to hold her again…

'Hey, Sam,' he said softly. 'How are you doing? Better?' He took the little hand in his, automatically noting that he was losing the chubby baby-fat look in favour of a typical little boy's hands…covered in nicks and scrapes from his latest adventure in their garden.

'I hope you've been thinking about that project,' he continued, as he cradled the slender fingers in his own hand, knowing he needed to keep his thoughts away from Kat until he could get his brain working properly again.

'You know, the one we were talking about before you had your operation?' he went on. 'Well, I had a look at that tree at the end of the garden—the one you suggested in the far right-hand corner—and I think it's going to be perfect for a tree-house.'

Ben smiled when he remembered the way the anaesthetist had scowled at him when he'd first brought the topic up, but Sam had seemed so small and defenceless and frightened lying there. He'd had to think of something for him to focus on to take his mind off what was about to happen but he certainly hadn't expected Sam to get so excited that he had been ready to leap off the trolley there and then to get started.

Now he wondered whether the suggestion had been wise. Had he been setting the boy up for disappointment? Was Sam ever going to be well enough to be able to help build it? Would he still have the co-ordination to be able to climb up into it? Just how much damage *had* the operation done to his brain?

He drew in a deep shuddering breath and then released Sam's hand hurriedly when he realised that his own hands were trembling visibly.

'Dear God,' he whispered in shock, wondering why he hadn't realised sooner just how much this little boy had come to mean to him. And Kat? Did he love her, too? Was *that* the reason why he'd lost his self-control and every inhibition he'd ever known?

No! He couldn't possibly be falling in love with Kat! He loved Lorraine. He'd *always* love Lorraine as long as he lived—

'Is there a problem, sir?' asked a worried voice, and he jerked round to face the nurse standing beside him.

'A problem?' he echoed blankly, still reeling from his convoluted thoughts.

'With Sam?' She gestured towards the silent figure. 'You were staring at him as if—'

'No!' he interrupted hastily, hoping she hadn't been watching when he'd been remembering when he and Kat had… 'No. Everything seems to be going well,' he said with a smile. Over her shoulder he caught sight of a clock and suddenly realised just how long he must have been sitting there. He would only just have time to get to the surgery on time for the start of the morning session. How could he not have noticed when the young woman had come in to do Sam's observations earlier? Had he been so lost in his thoughts?

But the lateness of the hour gave him the ideal excuse to escape.

'Time to go,' he said briskly, as he stood up and placed his chair out of the way against the wall. 'I'll be back later when the test results are in.' That would be when the decision had to be made whether it was time to lessen the drugs keeping Sam unconscious…when they would finally find out how successful the operation had been.

CHAPTER NINE

'HAS my first patient arrived already?' Ben asked Rose as he came in the door, and Kat's heart gave a crazy leap inside her in spite of the fact that he'd barely acknowledged her.

She turned her head away so neither their receptionist nor the man who'd caused it would see the accompanying flush of colour sweeping up her throat and into her face.

'Yes and no,' Rose said cryptically. 'I'd booked the K's to see you, but they decided they'd rather stick with Dr Leeman.'

'The Kays?' He frowned, holding out his hand for the thickly stuffed envelopes that contained the patients' notes. 'That name doesn't ring a bell.'

Kat couldn't help chuckling.

'Everyone calls them the K's not just because their surname is Kennedy but because their first names are...'

Before she could start the litany, the family in question chimed in for her. 'Kenneth, Kerry, Keith, Kieran and Kelvin!'

'We're not late, are we?' Kerry Kennedy asked while she tried frantically to keep her brood under control. 'We're bound to be. Ever since the boys arrived, we're permanently late for everything.'

'Not this time,' Kat reassured her, then glanced across at

Ben, wondering if the butterflies were going to swoop inside her every time she looked at him. 'If you don't mind me taking over today?'

'It's not that we've got anything against you, Doc,' Kenneth said hastily. 'It's just that we've known Dr Leeman ever since the two of them joined the practice and she was able to help us find out that we needed IVF to have this lot.'

'Triplets!' Ben exclaimed, as he waved away any objection, his tone seeming to come halfway between awe at the fact that they were so alike and horror at the thought of dealing with three such supercharged little bodies on a day-by-day basis.

'They're a bit like London buses. You wait for ages and then a whole bunch arrives all at once,' Kenneth explained wryly. 'We'd been married for five years and had virtually given up hope when the doc suggested we go for tests and we were offered IVF.'

'Well, you certainly hit the jackpot!' Ben exclaimed. 'Most people don't even get one.'

'We console ourselves with the thought that we're getting the hard part over all at once,' Kerry said wearily.

'So, which one of you am I seeing today?' Kat asked, as she turned to lead the way along the corridor.

'Most of us,' Kenneth said wryly, as he shepherded his sons in front of him. 'I'm just here to sit on the boys while you take a look at them, then I'll take them out to the waiting room while Kerry has a bit of privacy with you, if that's all right?'

'So, boys,' she said, when they were all stood in a row in front of her desk. 'What have you been up to?'

'We got *spots*!' announced one of them. Kat had never managed to sort out which name went with which child.

'Yeah! *Lotth* of thpoth!' agreed another, his speech hampered by two missing teeth right at the front.

'Look!' demanded the third, dragging up his clothing to display a very spotty tummy.

'Lots!' Kat agreed when she came round her desk to crouch in front of them for a closer look, but there wasn't any doubt in her mind what she was looking at. This wasn't the first case she'd seen in the last few weeks. 'It's chickenpox,' she announced as she straightened up. 'There's a lot of it going around the schools and playgroups at the moment. It happens every three or four years.'

'Obviously, that means we'll have to keep them home from school, but do they need to go to bed?' Kerry asked with an air of resignation.

'Not unless they're feeling particularly miserable or their temperature goes up,' Kat reassured her. 'Many children sail through it without a problem, especially fit healthy young men like yours. Your only problem is going to be stopping them from scratching,' she said, with a pointed glare at one of the triplets who was vigorously scratching his tummy through his clothing. 'Otherwise the spots can become infected and that can lead to other problems.'

She turned to check the filing stack on the cupboard behind her only to see that the pigeonhole marked 'Chickenpox' was empty.

'When you go out to Reception, ask for one of the leaflets about chickenpox and it will give you all the right information about when they'll be safe to go back to school and also advice about what to use to minimise the itching.'

'Thanks very much,' Kenneth said, but he looked rather shell-shocked at the prospect of three sick children. 'I'll go and get that while Kerry has a word with you.' He turned to the boys. 'Right, gang! Quick march to the door and no running!'

'He might as well have saved his breath,' Kerry said, as the sound of three sets of thundering feet diminished rapidly down the corridor. 'They don't do anything by halves.'

'So what can I do for you?' Kat asked. 'You're not going down with it, too?' She smiled at her patient but was mentally crossing her fingers. Chickenpox in an adult was a far more serious—even fatal—illness.

'Not me! I had it as a child and I've still got some of the scars to prove it,' she joked, pulling up a sleeve to point to one of the characteristic circular scars on the underside of her wrist. 'I've just been feeling generally out of sorts for the last couple of weeks and I didn't know whether I'd picked up some bug or something…in my waterworks or my stomach.'

Kat questioned her closely about the symptoms and onset and kept coming back to the one diagnosis that it *couldn't* be. Still, she thought as she sent Kerry off to provide a specimen of urine, stranger things *had* happened.

The result of the test was completely unequivocal but so unexpected that Kat did it twice before she turned to the waiting woman.

'Kerry, I don't know whether this is going to be good news or bad, but…you're pregnant.'

'Pregnant!' Kerry gasped, her mouth gaping in shock. 'But I *can't* be. *You* know how difficult it was for me to get pregnant, even with the IVF. It's… I'm…' She sat shaking her head, completely unable to utter another word.

Kat had an idea and reached for the phone. 'Rose, is Ben free?'

'He will be, any minute now,' the cheerful receptionist said over the sound of childish high jinks in the reception area. 'Did you want him to come to your room?'

'Could you ask him to keep an eye on triple trouble out there for a couple of minutes while you send Mr Kennedy back into my room?' Kat asked, wondering just what Ben would make of his childminding duties. He'd managed well with Josh and Sam but they were definitely less of a handful than the junior K's.

It was less than a minute before Kenneth was knocking on her door, but it had given Kerry enough time to catch her breath.

'Is there a problem, Doc?' he demanded, his forehead creased with worry as he hurried across to his wife. 'The other doctor said you wanted to see me.'

'It's not a problem exactly,' Kat began, but Kerry obviously didn't believe in beating about the bush.

'She says I'm pregnant!' she exclaimed with a sob that couldn't decide whether it was laughter or tears. 'She did the test twice, and each time…'

'Bloody hell!' Kenneth swore, and sat down in a hurry as every ounce of colour disappeared from his face. 'Sorry for swearing, Doc, but tell me it's not triplets again!'

'We won't know until Kerry has a scan, but to put your mind at rest we'll send her to the top of the queue, just so we know what we're dealing with.'

'And how soon will they be able to tell the sex of the baby?' Kerry asked, with sudden hope on her face. 'It would be great not to be the only female in the house.'

It was several more minutes before the two of them were

ready to face the world and relieve Ben of his childminding detail.

Kat couldn't help following the two of them out to the reception area, just to see how he'd managed with the rambunc-
tious trio, expecting to see every toy thrown out of the box
and littered around the room.

Instead, peace reigned, with three little boys sitting in a
row, absolutely spellbound while Ben read them the story of
the three billy goats gruff.

'Wow!' murmured Kerry, wide-eyed with amazement as
she took in the picture-perfect scene. 'Can we take him
home with us?'

The next time Kat saw Ben as anything more than a blur in
the distance was several days later when he was on his way
into the practice just as she was on her way out. The timing
couldn't have been more perfect.

'Oh, Ben!' she bubbled excitedly, flinging her arms around
him and squeezing him tight even as she fought off the tears
of relief. 'The hospital just rang. Sam's awake! Come on!'

She tugged at him, expecting him to follow her out
towards the car, but he stayed where he was as though
planted in the ground.

'I'll visit him later,' he said sombrely. 'I've got something… Ah, Kat, I can't…I need to have a word with you.
Preferably straight away.'

She didn't know why, but her heart suddenly sank with the
weight of premonition.

Just a moment ago her feet had barely touched the ground,
she'd been so excited about Sam's return to consciousness.
Now there was a terrible feeling of dread when she gazed up

into his shuttered face, and it was made worse by the fact that the haunted look had returned to his eyes.

'Couldn't we talk on the way to the hospital?' she suggested, still desperate to see for herself that Sam was really on the mend. 'I'm hoping to get there in time to catch Mr Rossiter. I need to thank him for what he's done for Sam.'

'I'm… He's…' Ben shook his head and gave a huff of frustration. 'Look, Kat, I know this is the worst possible time to spring this on you, but…'

Her feelings about this conversation grew immeasurably worse when she realised that he couldn't even bring himself to meet her eyes any more. Did he really regret their intimacy so much that he would…?

'You want to leave!' she blurted out, knowing she couldn't sidestep what was obviously about to happen. 'You want to leave the practice! While everything's so…' Panic clawed at her. 'Ben, you can't! Not when I need…*we* need—you so much!' Had he noticed her slip of the tongue? The last thing he needed if he was uncomfortable about having slept with her was to find out that she was falling in love with him.

'What about the practice? Your patients?' she continued urgently. 'I can't possibly manage it all on my own, not while I'm visiting Sam.'

'I've had a word with Simon this morning and he confirmed that he was only doing the locum work until he could find a practice he really liked. The three months I promised you ends this week and he's quite happy to take up the slack until you decide what you want to do, but he'd be keen to join the practice full time as soon as you like.'

He'd barely drawn a breath while he'd laid all the facts out, proving that this certainly hadn't been a snap decision. He'd already made all his arrangements.

Was there *nothing* she could do to change his mind? It was *Ben* she wanted to work with, not Simon Throssel, good though he was.

One look at Ben's face told her that she may as well save her breath. He'd made his decision and she had no one to blame but herself.

If she hadn't been so….needy.

If she hadn't…if *they* hadn't…

And every day since, she'd seen him becoming more and more withdrawn, until he'd returned to the sombre man he'd been the first time she'd met him.

'I need to ask you a favour,' he continued, and she nearly laughed aloud at the incongruity of the request. Didn't he know that she would do *anything* for him? 'Would it be all right for me to leave some of my stuff here to be collected later, when I know where I'm going and what I'm doing?'

'Oh, Ben,' she breathed, the threat of tears scalding her eyes and distorting her view of his face until it almost looked as if he *could* tell how much she was hurting and shared her pain.

'Kat? Haven't you gone to the hospital yet?' called Rose, sticking her head out of the window. 'You were going to try to catch the surgeon, remember?'

'I'm going, Rose,' she called back with a wave, hoping the receptionist couldn't hear that her voice was thick with repressed tears. 'I got sidetracked on the way to the car. I'll see you when I get back.'

'You don't have to worry about him any more, Kat,' Ben said, as she finally forced herself to turn towards her car, lost for words now that she knew his decision was irrevocable. 'Sam's going to be all right. You'll see.'

Kat couldn't help sitting in her car for a moment to watch Ben's familiar long-legged stride taking him into the practice and out of her sight. She was so glad that Josh was at school that day because she had no idea how she was going to tell him that Ben was leaving. After his initial wariness towards the man, he'd gradually opened up until he was almost the carefree youngster he'd been before Richard had died. He was going to be devastated when he heard. She was just going to have to hope that she found the right words to explain it to him by the time he came home from school.

Sam was a different matter. He'd accepted Ben with all the open-hearted generosity of a friendly puppy, blossoming under his praise and guidance. He would be expecting his idol to be there when he finally came out of hospital.

In fact, she realised that their whole little family was going to be devastated by Ben's announcement, and it took all her determination to bottle up her tears and make herself drive to the hospital. Today was the day when she would discover just how well Sam's operation had gone and once again she was going to have to cope all on her own. She couldn't afford to be weak, not when Sam needed her to be strong.

'Hi, Mum,' Sam croaked as soon he saw her, his voice sounding almost rusty but his blue eyes…Richard's eyes…were as bright as ever since the operation had removed the pressure on the optic nerve and ensured his sight.

'Hello, sunshine. How are you feeling?' She came very close to losing control of the tears when she saw him lying there, propped up against a bank of pillows like some pampered potentate. It felt so very good to wrap him in her arms and hold him again.

'Is Ben coming soon?' he demanded eagerly, giving his usual wriggle of discomfort when she held him too long for his boyish sensibilities. 'Did you know he was there for my operation? Did you know they did it all up my nose? All those tubes and…and things! I want to ask him what it was like.'

Kat remembered hearing Ben's voice when he'd spoken to Sam before he'd gone into Theatre. She'd always be grateful that he'd kept his promise to be there for her son, even though he was going to let him down now.

'He probably won't be able to tell you exactly what went on in the operation because he wasn't there when they were doing it,' she pointed out, determined to think only of the fact that, so far, it seemed as if Sam had come through the operation with flying colours. Hopefully she wouldn't have to wait too long before someone let her know all the details of the diagnosis and prognosis.

'He *was* there,' Sam argued adamantly, even though the residual effects of the drugs were making him visibly sleepy. 'He was talking to me about building a tree-house in the big tree at the bottom of the garden. Him and me are going to design it, but we'll prob'ly let Josh help us to build it, too.'

'That'll be good,' Kat agreed with an attempt at a smile that he didn't see, his eyes finally giving up the battle to stay open. She closed her own, wondering how on earth she was going to be able to fulfil Sam's dream of having a tree-house, now that Ben was leaving. All the while it had just been something in his own head, she'd been able to do the 'we'll see' delaying tactic that all children recognised. Now that Ben had discussed it with him in detail, he was obviously expecting it to materialise in a matter of days, and that was something she couldn't promise.

For now, she was just going to have to take each day as it came. It was far too soon after the operation for Sam to be given the devastating news that Ben was leaving. Perhaps, if he didn't see him while he was in the hospital, the hero-worship might have a little time to subside and the blow wouldn't be so severe.

The reception area was already starting to fill up for evening surgery by the time she returned from the hospital, and the phone was ringing.

Kat pulled a wry face. The castles she'd been tentatively building in the air may have come tumbling down this morning, but the world was continuing to turn in its usual way.

'Oh, good! You're back,' exclaimed Rose, holding out the phone towards her with an eager expression on her face. 'This one's for you. It's Mrs K!'

Kat hurried to take the receiver from her, wondering whether one of the triplets might be reacting badly to the chickenpox virus. The illness was usually fairly benign in children, but there was always the chance of febrile convulsions if the child's temperature rose too fast.

'Mrs Kennedy, this is Dr Leeman. What can I do for you?'

'Absolutely nothing, except raise a glass!' Kerry said, and just from those few words Kat could tell that she must be grinning from ear to ear.

'Do I take it you've had your scan?' she guessed.

'About an hour ago,' she confirmed. 'When I phoned up

to make the appointment, I mentioned that we'd had triplets the last time and they fitted me in today.'

'And?' Kat prompted, no doubt in her mind that her diagnosis had been correct.

'And it's *twins*!' she exclaimed, and it was difficult to tell whether she was more delighted than horrified or vice versa. 'Doctor, I don't understand. How on earth could this happen when we had to have IVF the first time?'

'I'll be perfectly honest with you, Mrs Kennedy,' Kat said. 'I've absolutely no idea. You'll have to ask your obstetrician when you see him.'

'I think Kenneth's going to be doing that,' she said wryly. 'At the moment he's sitting here looking like a stunned mullet and muttering "At least it's only two this time" over and over.'

Kat laughed. 'Well, at least he's got a few months to get used to the idea.'

'And to build on another bedroom to put them in,' her patient added. 'Once the boys get a bit bigger, they'll need more space, too. We're going to have to start looking for a stately home to get enough bedrooms at this rate! At least the boys will be at school full time by the time these two arrive.'

'Were they able to tell the sex of the babies from the scan or did you decide to wait till they arrive to find out this time?'

'I wanted to know straight away, but the two of them weren't being co-operative,' she grumbled.

'You might have better luck next time,' Kat pointed out. 'Anyway, the most important thing is that they're healthy.'

As Kerry confirmed that all was well so far, Kat caught sight of the clock. She grimaced and brought the conversation to a speedy close, suddenly realising that it was already time to see her first patient. She'd hoped she would have a chance for a word with Ben, to ask him about the tree-house that he'd been planning with Sam, but there wouldn't be time now. She would have to wait until the end of surgery to catch him.

'Why is it that the one day you want to finish on time, everything goes pear-shaped?' Kat muttered, as she shut down her computer and retrieved her bag from the locked drawer in her desk.

As she carried the basket of patient files towards the reception area, she was surprised to hear Josh's voice floating along the corridor.

'Hi, Mum. Ready to go home?' he asked, as he stacked a couple of books and slid them inside his backpack.

'Hello, Josh. What are you doing over here?' The boys hadn't had to wait for her in the practice for months…ever since Ben had joined the practice, in fact. As sensible as Josh was, she really didn't think it was right for him to have the responsibility of looking after his young brother alone, even though the practice was within shouting distance.

'Ben told me to come over,' Josh said blithely. 'He said he had to go out and he knew you don't like Sam and me staying in the house alone.'

'Ben's gone out?' she said with a sudden sense of panic, silently scolding herself for her stupidity. The last time she'd raced up those spiral stairs to see if he'd left the practice, it had been a false alarm. This time would be no different.

'He said he'd told you about it earlier today,' Josh continued, obviously completely unconcerned by the message as he slung the rucksack over one shoulder and held the door open for her. 'Do you know when he'll be back? I wanted to show him the biology test we had today. I got top marks in the whole class after he explained it to me so I could understand. I just didn't get it when the teacher told us.'

Kat managed to find the right motherly words of congratulations for his achievement but all the time she was silently repeating Josh's words…*he said he'd told you about it*…when the only thing she and Ben had spoken about was the fact that he was going to leave.

The emotional, needy part of her wanted to race inside and up the stairs to check whether Ben had really gone without another word, but she had a son to feed, his homework to supervise and then she was taking him to visit Sam.

And there really wasn't any point in looking upstairs, she realised once she'd opened the front door and stepped inside. There was something so *empty* about the silent house that she just knew Ben had gone for good.

Kat propped her head in her hands, only just resisting the urge to rub her burning eyes when she remembered that it would make a mess of her minimal eye make-up. She didn't need to look any more like a panda. Her sleepless nights had given her such dark circles under her eyes that they looked almost like bruises.

It was going to be so hard to keep her mind on her patients when all she could do was endlessly wonder what she could have done differently. It was a bit difficult to decide when she didn't know what she'd said or done to drive him away.

'I thought he was happy, spending time with us,' she murmured, her heart heavy when she remembered how well he'd fitted in with her little family. He'd certainly looked a lot happier than when he'd arrived…right until that night.

Was *that* what had made him decide to leave? Had he realised that he couldn't live in her house any more, not when he was going to be seeing the woman who had made him betray his wife's memory?

If, as she suspected, she'd been the first person he'd opened up to, it was a given that he hadn't even started to get over his loss. His feeling of guilt would have automatically made him blame her.

And she was a fool if she was clinging to the fact that he'd left most of his belongings in the room upstairs as a guarantee that she'd see him at least once more. He'd packed everything and left it piled beside the top of the spiral staircase, so it was just as likely that he'd organise a commercial carrier to pick up the boxes for him.

It was definitely time to get her act together, no matter how much she was hurting. Especially as the chickenpox epidemic showed no sign of diminishing yet. The practice had been inundated with calls from anxious parents and with her hours of patient contact curtailed by her need to spend time with Sam at the hospital and with Josh at home...

The phone rang again and she groaned, but at least it had stopped the endless circle of her thoughts.

'Dr Leeman, Mr Khan would like to have a word with you, if you're free,' Rose announced formally.

'Mr Khan?' She couldn't remember a patient with that name, but it did seem familiar.

'The orthopaedic surgeon you sent Mr Aldarini to,' Rose reminded her helpfully.

'Oh, yes!' Kat exclaimed. 'Please, put the call through.'

'Actually, he's not on the phone,' she said with an unexpected air of excitement to her tone. 'He's here in Reception.'

'Well, in that case, I'll come out,' she said cheerfully, and it was only when she put the receiver down that she remembered what a mess she looked that morning. 'Oh, help!' she squeaked, scrabbling for the key to unlock the desk drawer while she crossed her fingers that she'd at least put a hairbrush and a tube of lipstick in it that morning.

Two frantic minutes later she was giving a tug to the hem of her jacket and striding along the corridor, hoping she didn't look a disgrace to the practice.

'Mr Khan,' she said with a smile as she entered the reception area, and the elegant-looking gentleman who had been inspecting the toys in the children's corner straightened up and turned to return the smile with a blinding one of his own.

He was younger than she'd expected, and quite ridiculously good-looking with his dark soulful eyes and skin that looked as if it had a permanent deep gold tan.

'Please, if it would not offend you, you could call me Razak,' he invited in a voice so soft and rich that it made her think of being wrapped in dark brown velvet.

'And I'm Kat,' she responded, offering him her hand even as she wondered why such a stunning example of manhood was having so little effect on her, whereas Ben...

'Cat, like the animal?' he enquired, with a blink of surprise.

'No.' She chuckled. 'Kat, short for Katriona. Would you like to take a seat? I'm sure Rose wouldn't mind making us some coffee.' In fact, if Rose leant any closer to follow their conversation, she would tumble head first over the reception counter. Already Kat could see that her matchmaking antennae were quivering with excitement.

'No coffee, thank you. I was driving in this direction, exploring your beautiful country, and decided to call into your surgery when I recognised the address. I don't want to take up too much of your time,' he added easily. 'Your Rose has already told me how busy you are with your son in hospital. It is good news that his operation has gone well.'

'The best,' Kat agreed wholeheartedly. 'Unless you've gone through something like that, knowing that there's a danger that your child is going to be seriously disabled by an operation but that if he *doesn't* have the surgery, he'll probably die…' She shook her head wordlessly, knowing she would never be able to thank Mr Rossiter enough for giving Sam back to her.

'My patients aren't usually in that life-or-death situation,' he admitted self-deprecatingly. 'Mostly, they are just pleased to be out of pain at last, those who have replacement joints, like your Mr Aldarini.'

'I did wonder if that was why you were here, but…has there been a problem that you needed to come here in person?'

'No problem at all,' he reassured her with another of those brilliant smiles, his delicious accent almost musical on her ears. 'Mr Aldarini is only partly why I am here. He is recovering well, in spite of the fact he delayed having the operation for far too long. Mostly, I wanted to tell you that, with the tandem system trial at the hospital, we are managing to do many more operations than before, but I will only be here for a few more months before I return to my own country to set up a whole new department. So I will need all the practice I can get and I wanted to let you know that if you have any more patients in your practice who are in a similar position or whose operations have been delayed unnecessarily, I would be willing for you to refer them to me directly.'

Kat blinked in surprise. Usually she referred to the department and had little input as to which of the orthopaedic surgeons would eventually do the operation—hopefully, the one with the shortest list. It had been a one-off inspiration that had had her contacting Mr Khan's receptionist in the hope that he hadn't already inherited an enormous back list of people waiting impatiently for their operations to take place.

'Won't your superiors have something to say about that?' she queried warily. After all, she was going to have to continue to deal with the orthopaedic department long after Razak had returned to his own country. She couldn't afford to put anyone's nose out of joint.

'It will not be a problem,' he reassured her easily. 'They still work in their old way and have more patients waiting than they can manage, with waiting lists that stretch…' He demonstrated with his arms spread wide, almost like a fisherman describing the one that got away.

Kat thanked him sincerely for his offer but as he made his farewells, she wondered when she would find the time to go through her patient files to pull out the ones who would benefit from his suggestion. She would *have* to find the time somehow—it was too good an offer to turn down, especially for those patients who were already crippled by the pain of their condition.

'Now, that was one very handsome man!' Rose exclaimed almost as soon as the door closed behind him. 'And I think he liked you, too.'

'He seems very nice,' Kat agreed. 'But you heard him say that he'll be going back home in a matter of months, so there's no point in getting your hopes up…unless you *want* me to leave the country?' she teased.

Another man who'll be here and then gone, just when he's made himself indispensable, she thought as Rose stifled her rebuttal to answer another phone call.

Kat waited long enough to know that it wasn't a call that needed her immediate attention then gave Rose a wave and gestured to let her know she was going. She hurried round to the house for a flying visit, knowing that she needed to grab a bite to eat before she went to the hospital to spend some time with Sam.

She could hear her private line ringing as she put her key in the lock and nearly tripped over the threshold in her hurry to get to it in time, suddenly hopeful that she'd hear Ben's voice on the other end.

'Is my daddy there?' demanded a tearful voice at the other end of the line, one that sounded as if it belonged to a young girl, if Kat wasn't mistaken.

'I think you might have dialled a wrong number,' she suggested gently. 'Do you know what number it was you wanted?'

'Aren't you Dr Leeman?' the youngster pleaded. 'Daddy gave me this number.'

'I'm Dr Leeman, but—' Kat began.

'Well, then, that's where my daddy's working because he told me about living with you. He said you're called Kat and…and you've got two boys called Josh and Sam and…and I've been trying to phone him to tell him I need to go home, but I can't *find* him!'

For several moments Kat hadn't been able to process what she was hearing, but all of a sudden the penny dropped and she found herself staring at the receiver in shock. She was speaking to someone she hadn't even known existed— Ben's daughter.

CHAPTER TEN

THE child on the other end of the line had carried on speaking as Kat was reeling with disbelief. It had taken him long enough to tell her that he'd been married, but Ben had never so much as *mentioned* that he had a daughter.

'I've been trying to talk to him to tell him I've got chickenpox,' she continued tearfully, 'but he's not answering his phone and…and Matron says I can come home because the infirmary is full…but I don't know where he is and…and he gave me this number and…'

That makes two of us who don't know where he is, Kat thought, but there was a more immediate problem to solve with a distraught child.

'Shh! Sweetheart, shh!' Kat soothed. 'Take a deep breath and tell me your name.'

'L-Laura,' she hiccuped.

'L-Laura?' Kat mimicked, and was rewarded by a watery giggle, but it was a start. 'Is there someone I could talk to at the school to find out—?'

'Matron's here,' Laura broke in. 'I'm using her phone…' Her voice faded, to be replaced by a pleasantly motherly one.

'Dr Leeman? I'm Joan Coriffis, matron at St Bernard's. Is there any way you could contact Laura's father to tell him she needs collecting? I need to ask the parents who live closest to the school if they can take their daughters so I can care properly for the ones whose parents are abroad. I had a big family of my own before I returned to being a matron, but caring for dozens at a time is proving a real headache.'

Kat had heard of St Bernard's—a good boarding school not too far away, and probably the reason why Ben had applied for the job at Ditchling.

Kat could only imagine how miserable Laura was feeling, and how alone with her father out of contact. She made a snap decision.

'Matron, I can't contact Laura's father immediately, but if I were to come to the school later this afternoon, do you think it would be in order for me to collect her and bring her home to look after her?'

There was an uncomfortable pause on the other end of the phone, one that Kat completely understood in view of the strict regulations most schools now insisted on for the safety of the pupils in their charge. Then, in the background, she heard another voice calling the matron's name to inform her that they had another two patients and it seemed as if the decision was made.

'If you bring some identification with you and some proof that Laura's father actually works at your practice,' she suggested hurriedly. 'Bring it up to the infirmary... The school secretary will direct you...' The voice behind the matron became suddenly urgent. 'I'm sorry, but I'll have to go. I'll see you soon, Dr...'

The phone clattered down before she'd even managed to

recall Kat's name, but Kat could hardly blame the woman. It had been bad enough in the practice, seeing them in ones and twos…and threes in the case of the K's! She couldn't imagine how the poor woman was coping with dozens.

The rest of the afternoon passed in a blur of activity, starting with a moment of blind panic before she checked her textbook and realised that the dangerous connection she'd made in her head between the corticosteroids Sam had received and Laura's chickenpox was unimportant because Sam had already had the virus.

Everything else was pure practicality, from making Ben's bed up with pretty sheets to asking Rose to keep an eye out for Josh in case he arrived home from school before Kat returned from collecting Laura. And somewhere in the middle of it all, she'd managed to spend an hour with Sam, who was actually starting to grow bored with the inactivity—even the computer games—and was campaigning to go home.

'As if I haven't got enough on my plate without taking on extra…' Kate muttered as she followed the school secretary's directions towards the infirmary. 'I must be completely mad!' But then she saw the spotty little waif waiting for her, looking up at her with Ben's beautiful green eyes, and she knew she was doing the right thing.

'Are you Kat?' the young girl asked shyly, a slender little thing at eleven years old, who was obviously going to be every bit as beautiful as her mother in a few years.

'Dr Leeman,' the matron corrected her swiftly even as she cast a cursory glance over the identification Kat had handed her as soon as they met.

'But Kat will do for now,' Kat added, as she took in the

slightly hectic flush and over-bright eyes that signalled a raised temperature. It was time they were on their way. The sooner Laura was tucked up in bed again, the better. 'Has someone collected her wash kit and some clothing, so we can be on our way?'

'I packed my bag myself,' Laura offered with a shy smile. 'I wanted to choose my favourite books and clothes.'

'Good thinking!' Kat smiled, then turned to Kate Coriffis again. 'So, are you happy for me to take charge of Laura in her father's absence?'

Her question was almost lost under the sound of knuckles rapping urgently on the door and a young voice calling for the matron.

'Yes. Of course,' she agreed hastily, almost thrusting Kat's ID into her hands to end the conversation. 'And I'll leave it to Mr Rossiter to let us know when Laura is well enough to return to school.'

Kat blinked when she heard the name, startled that it was the same as Sam's elusive surgeon, and had to stifle a smile. If Matron was getting the children's names wrong like that, she was obviously being run ragged by the epidemic.

Well, Laura would no longer be one of dozens needing attention once she got her settled at Ditchling. *She* would be able to look after her with all the care that her mother, Lorraine, would have lavished on her.

Ironically, Kat remembered that she'd actually been trying to persuade Richard to have another child when he'd become ill. She would have to be careful not to give in to the temptation to treat Laura as a surrogate for the daughter she'd always wanted to have.

Now all she'd have to do was work out how she was going

to fit a full day's work in with full-time mothering of a sick child *and* visiting Sam during his recovery in hospital.

In the event, everything went so smoothly that Kat ended up walking around, waiting for the other shoe to drop.

The fact that it was a weekend helped, as had the fact that Josh had displayed none of his prickly wariness towards Laura, possibly because she was so appreciative whenever he did anything for her. Laura herself was feeling so much better that within two days she was well enough to join them downstairs for most of the day.

Best of all, Sam's recovery after the operation had been so spectacular that he was ready to come home far sooner than she could ever have hoped, with his sight back to normal and his headaches gone.

'It looks as if it's been a complete success,' Jon Fox-Croft exulted when he showed her the latest set of tests. 'He's been a very lucky little boy, especially to have someone of the calibre of Ben Rossiter willing to do his operation.'

Kat knew that Sam wasn't completely out of the woods yet. He would have to have regular check-ups as there was always the possibility of a recurrence, but so far…

Her only disappointment was that, wherever he was now, Ben hadn't even bothered to ring to find out how Sam was progressing. She'd been so certain that he cared enough about her son to make some sort of contact. Still, with Laura living with them, she was guaranteed to see him at least once more, when he came to pick up his daughter. *That* was when she was going to ask him why he'd never told her about Laura.

It couldn't be because he was ashamed of her because she was a lovely girl, bright and intelligent…clearly doing well at school in spite of the fact that she didn't want to be a boarder.

'Josh and Sam are so lucky,' she'd sighed wistfully earlier on that evening when Kat had been chivvying the boys into clearing the table after their meal. 'I'd like to live with my dad and go to a day school again.' She glanced up at Kat, as though gauging her reaction. 'I know it sounds stupid to say I'm lonely when there are so many people at school, but I miss him.'

And that was something else she was going to tell the man when he finally turned up—the fact that his daughter needed him to be more than an intermittent visitor in her life.

In the meantime, it was Sunday evening and she desperately needed to deal with the laundry, or Josh would be going to school in his scruffy jeans while Sam and Laura would have to stay in their pyjamas.

'Laura, sweetheart, can you sort out the clothes you'd like washed so I can get them in the machine? You, too, Josh. Just do a quick check that all the socks made it into the basket, please. Don't leave any to fester under the bed.'

'But Laura was just going to play against me on the computer,' he moaned, and her heart lifted to hear him behaving like a completely normal child again. Would he revert to the withdrawn worrier of the last year when she finally had to tell him that Ben was only going to be returning long enough to retrieve his daughter and his belongings—that he'd already left them?

'Come on, Josh, I'll race you,' Laura challenged, and sprinted towards the spiral staircase, and Kat's heart lifted at the sound of such innocent childish rivalry, making her determined to enjoy it while she could.

* * *

'I'm sorry, Lorraine,' Ben whispered, as he crouched by her headstone in the gathering dusk, his first tears a mixture of fire and ice as they trickled down his cheeks. 'Sorry I made so many mistakes…so many stupid decisions.' He reached out to trace her name with an unsteady fingertip.

The stone was still so fresh and new, the incised words so sharp that they looked as if they'd only been completed yesterday.

'I know that I couldn't have stopped the cancer killing you in the end, but if I'd recognised how serious…' He shook his head. He would always regret the fact that they'd been robbed of the chance to say a proper goodbye, that he would never be sure, once she'd lapsed into a coma, that she'd heard him tell her how much he loved her…would *always* love her.

It was Kat and her two boys who had made him realise that withdrawing inside himself wasn't doing anyone any good, especially when Sam had become ill. His insides still cramped with something like fear when he realised that it was his own special knowledge of the condition that had helped him make the diagnosis and secured the treatment the youngster had needed without delay.

'But how many others are there out there?' he whispered, for the first time in so long doubting the path he'd taken after Lorraine had died. Had he made a monumental mistake in turning away from the specialty that had left him too busy to notice that she was sick, too?

At least he hadn't failed Sam. It was early days yet, but it looked as if he was going to be one of the luckiest ones, with all the debilitating symptoms completely reversed by the removal of the tumour. He could only pray that the youngster's good luck held and that he had no recurrence in the months and years ahead.

And as for all those other children…all the other Sams who needed the same sort of luck…

'What should I do, love?' he whispered, but in his heart he knew that the decision was already made. The leaden feeling inside his chest was already lightening and warmth spread through him when Kat's face appeared in his mind's eye.

'I'll never forget you, Lorraine,' he said, his voice firmer and more assured as he recognised what he had to do. 'But…you would have liked Kat. She's very like you—hard-working, uncomplaining, loving. And her boys would have loved you as much as Laura does.' The picture in his head expanded to include his precious daughter, and for the first time he let himself think about the possibilities that might lie in the future.

'What a fool I've been!' he exclaimed aloud. What on earth had possessed him to think that taking a string of short-term posts as a locum GP would ever be enough for him? His skills lay in another direction entirely, and it was time he stopped wasting them…there were too many children who needed them.

He stroked his hand over the petals of the single red rose he'd placed at the foot of the headstone, pleased to see that it was now perfectly steady, as steady as it would need to be when he performed that most demanding of all specialities—neuro-surgery.

'It's time for me to go,' he said, as he scrubbed both hands over his face, a new determination in his voice. 'I'll never forget you, but I need to see Kat, to explain…to tell her that I…'

What?

That he'd finally got his head on straight?

'Yeah! That's about the size of it,' he said aloud, and with one last glance of farewell at the final resting place of the woman who would always occupy a corner of his heart, he started striding towards his car.

And then, at the thought that he was going back to Kat, walking wasn't nearly fast enough and he began to run.

The last person he'd expected to see when he let himself in the front door was his daughter, barrelling into the hallway from Kat's kitchen with Josh in hot pursuit.

'Dad!' she shrieked as soon as she caught sight of him, and launched herself into his arms. 'You're back!'

'I'm also deaf!' he complained, even as he relished the sensation of her arms wrapped tightly around him. When had she grown so tall? How had he missed noticing that she was growing so fast? Had he really been so wrapped up in his guilt that he'd forgotten to see that life was going on as usual all around him? And what on earth was she doing here, in Kat's house?

'I got chickenpox!' she announced, stating the obvious, the pale pink blotches of calamine lotion doing nothing to detract from her elfin beauty. 'And when you didn't answer your phone, I talked to Josh and Sam's mum and she spoke to Matron and she came to school to get me so I would be here when you got back.'

'Well, that certainly brings me up to date with events in my absence,' he said wryly, meeting Kat's wary gaze over his daughter's head.

'Oh, and, Dad, I've got a letter for you from Matron. I put it…' She wriggled out of his arms and went to the table in

he hallway where a complete assortment of objects always
seemed to come to rest— Kat's bag, ready for a call-out, of
course, and the car keys, a small pile of personal correspon-
dence and letters ready for posting. Laura had obviously
added her letter to the mix.

'Look at the envelope, Dad,' she said, holding it up to him
with a chuckle. 'She's put *Dr* Rossiter on it instead of *Mr*.
Doesn't she know that neurosurgeons are called Mr?'

He saw Kat's jaw drop and her eyes grow wide and
almost groaned aloud. He could almost hear her processing
the information.

Kat almost forgot to breathe.

His name was *Rossiter?* He was a *neurosurgeon? Sam's*
surgeon?

Had *anything* he'd told her been the truth? She didn't
even know his real *name*, for heaven's sake! Was he even a
GP or was she guilty of negligently employing an associate
who hadn't qualified to practice in this discipline?

Hot on the heels of her shock came anger, but when she
opened her mouth to explode he held her gaze and shook his
head with a look of stark pleading in those unforgettable
green eyes. She could almost hear him willing her to wait
until later, when the children wouldn't have to be witnesses
to their discussion.

'Hey, Dr Ben!' Sam called happily, as he joined them in
the hall, unwittingly breaking the sudden tension that
crackled in the air between the two of them. 'I told Mum you
were talking to me in the operating room…about the tree-
house. Will we be starting on it in the morning?'

'That's a weekend sort of job, Sam,' Ben explained,

without breaking the tenuous link with Kat for several long seconds, almost as though he was afraid to look away. 'We have to work during the week, but I haven't had a chance to talk about it with your mother to make sure…' He hesitated fractionally, as though choosing his words carefully. 'We have to make sure that she approves of our design and we haven't even put it on paper yet.'

'I'll do it now,' he volunteered eagerly.

'Not tonight, sunshine,' Kat decreed firmly. 'It's time you got ready for bed. And Josh needs to get his things ready for school tomorrow.' This sort of conversation was easy, normal, routine. This she could cope with. The conversation that would take place later was another matter and she didn't know whether her heart would ever recover from it.

Kat was hovering in the hallway when he finally came down the stairs, Laura settled on the hide-away bed that did duty when her boys had a visitor to stay.

She'd tried sitting in her favourite chair in the sitting room, but there was too much explosive tension boiling inside her to let her be still for long. Then she'd gone into the kitchen, but there'd been nothing left to do in there, not until the tumble-dryer finished its final load.

'Is there any chance of a cup of coffee?' Ben said, and when she suddenly realised that she didn't even know whether he was called Ben at all, she nearly lost it…until he added, 'I haven't had anything since breakfast in a B and B near where Lorraine's buried.'

She drew in a steadying breath as she took a closer look at him and realised it wasn't just that she was looking at him through suspicious eyes—there really *was* something different about him. He looked tired and rumpled from travelling, but for the first time since she'd met him there were no lingering shadows dulling those beautiful eyes. He even seemed somehow more *alive* than ever before, too.

'Have you eaten anything?' she asked, as she turned back into the kitchen, her nurturing instincts impossible to ignore.

It was the work of minutes to find a portion of home-made lasagne in the freezer and transfer it to the microwave while the kettle was boiling for two cups of instant coffee…decaffeinated seemed like a good idea when her nerves were this jangled.

Kat stood for a moment with her hands wrapped around the steaming mug, stupidly watching the turntable revolve while the microwave hummed, then couldn't stand the waiting any more.

'I can't do this!' she burst out, slamming the mug on the work surface so hard that it was a wonder that it didn't shatter. As it was, most of the contents erupted over the top to spread in a widening pool around it.

She whirled to face him, every molecule in her body shaking with the need to have some answers.

'How could you leave like that?' she demanded hoarsely. 'How could you just…go?'

'Because I'm a fool?' he said simply, and gave a wry smile. 'That's what I told Lorraine today when I— Oh,' he broke off, evidently realising that she'd been startled by the way the conversation had suddenly veered and needed an explanation. 'That's where I've been, Kat. I realised that I had some thinking to do, some ghosts to lay to rest and some decisions to make about the future.'

Her heart clenched with pain that he hadn't felt he could have done at least part of that list *here*, with her.

'Well, why don't you add a few more topics to that list?' she suggested sharply. 'Try…some apologies to make, some lies to explain and some explanations to give.' She glared at him. 'How about starting with your name? Is it Dr Benjamin Ross or Mr Benjamin Rossiter?'

'Both, in a way,' he equivocated. 'because once you've made a bit of a name for yourself, it's impossible to try to do anything else without people presuming that you've *got* to, that you might have been kicked out for negligence or… Oh, Kat, will you let me start at the beginning? Then you might be able to make sense of it.'

She nodded warily. 'But I reserve the right to ask questions.'

'Noted,' he agreed, then paused as though uncertain just where to start.

'Why not begin with the fact that your wife died and you put your daughter in a boarding school?' she suggested pointedly, then added, 'By the way, you're going to have a fight on your hands if you try to make her go back there. She said she hates it because she's lonely and she misses you. She wants to go to a school where she can come home at night, like Josh and Sam do.'

'I'd like that, too. I've missed her dreadfully,' he admitted. 'But all the time I was moving from pillar to post—taking on locum jobs or covering for someone's maternity leave or whatever—she needed the stability of staying put in one place. I couldn't keep dragging her around to a different school every time.'

'So why move around? And why the change to GP in the first place?' She pinned him with a searching look, certain she'd know if he wasn't telling her the truth.

'Guilt,' he said bluntly, and she believed him, knowing that feeling all too well. 'I felt so guilty that I hadn't been able to save my own wife that I lost it.' He thrust his hands into his pockets, his shoulders hunching defensively. 'I even thought of giving up medicine entirely, but I couldn't. It's all I've wanted to do since I was Laura's age.'

'So why retrain as a GP?'

'Because I thought I could do less damage there,' he admitted in a low voice. 'I'd be part of a team and if I had any doubts about a diagnosis, there'd be people I could turn to.'

'But—'

'It's different when you're a neurosurgeon,' he continued urgently, preventing her from interrupting his train of thought. 'Yes, you've got a full team of very experienced staff in Theatre and you've got all the fancy technology to help you, but when it's time to decide whether to pull back or to try to take out just a little more of a tumour to give the patient a better chance of survival, even though you know you're risking their eyesight, their ability to walk…even turning them into cabbages…when you know that you are the *only* person who can make that decision, and that if you get it wrong… And suddenly I just couldn't do it any more. I didn't trust my own judgement.'

'But you operated on Sam,' she pointed out through a throat so tight it was amazing that the words emerged. She'd never realised just how high-stress his job could be, and the fact that he'd gone through so much heart-searching alone when she would have been only too willing to…

'I couldn't *not* operate on him,' he said simply. 'I was pretty certain what was causing his symptoms but once he was diagnosed, I just couldn't pass him on for someone else to operate, not when it was so important that he had the best possible surgeon.'

'And modest, too!' she teased, and had to stifle a smile when she saw the embarrassed colour flood his face when he realised how his words had sounded. 'But I know what you mean. I looked you up on the Internet when I knew the name of Sam's surgeon and when it was over, I so wanted to meet you to thank you for what you'd done.'

'No thanks necessary,' Ben said, with a dismissive shake of his head. 'I'm just grateful that it turned out so well when I hadn't operated for so long. I was afraid that I was actually risking Sam's... But once I started, it was as if I'd never been away. It all came back—the concentration as you're feeling your way, trying to separate good tissue from bad without damaging anything irreplaceable was still there, and the sixth sense that seems to kick in while you're trying to decide if you've gone as far as you dare, or whether to dare a little more...'

'And you discovered you'd missed it,' Kat said, and it wasn't a question. Suddenly she had almost every answer she needed. She only had to see the expression on his face when he was talking about being a neurosurgeon, hear the fervour in his voice and the extra sparkle in his eyes. 'So you needed time to come to terms with the fact that your knee-jerk reaction to give it all up had been wrong. That, in spite of your misplaced guilt over Lorraine's death, you'd made a mistake in trying to force yourself to be a GP instead.'

'Exactly!' he said with bone-deep conviction. 'I realised that I wanted...*needed*...to return to neurosurgery and, yes, I realised that it had been a self-imposed exile but, no, it wasn't a mistake to become a GP or I'd never have met you and Josh and Sam. It might have taken me years to get my head together without this little family showing me what was important, and that certainly *wasn't* shutting the rest of the world out to wallow in guilt and misery.' He shrugged. 'I also realised that there are so many other Sams out there who need a chance at life, and there are never enough neurosurgeons.'

'Let alone *superb* neurosurgeons,' she ribbed him lightly, even though she'd never felt less light-hearted.

She really *was* going to lose him this time. He was going to be moving away permanently, taking Laura back home with him because his old hospital would welcome him back with open arms. While she…

'I've been offered a job at Sam's hospital,' he announced into the silence that she hadn't been able to bring herself to break. 'Jon Fox-Croft—you remember the neuro-radiologist who was part of the team—'

'And who ran interference for you so I wouldn't get to meet Mr Rossiter,' she interrupted, as another piece of the puzzle fell into place.

'I'd told him before I operated on Sam that I was far from certain that I wanted to go back to surgery, but once I was back in Theatre it was…as if I'd never been away. And Jon knew it and pointed out that they were wanting to expand the department to make it into a centre of excellence that would take children from all over the country…'

'And are you thinking of accepting?' She hardly dared breathe as she waited for his answer, the sudden hope almost too much to bear. If he did, he and Laura would still be close enough to stay in contact, but could she cope with that when she wanted so much more?

'On one condition,' he said seriously, crossing the few feet of kitchen floor that had separated them for the whole of their conversation. He stopped just tempting inches away from her to continue, his voice low and husky. 'I love you, Kat, and I need to know that I haven't completely blotted my copybook. That there's a possibility that, at some time in the future, you could forgive me and fall in love with me, too, and that you'd be willing to be a mother to Laura.'

'I already love Laura,' she admitted easily, as her heart took flight with the realisation that everything she wanted was within her grasp. 'She's the daughter I always wanted— bright, happy and loving, even when she's feeling miserable with chickenpox.'

'And Laura's father?' he prompted, with just a shadow of uncertainty darkening those beautiful green eyes.

Would any child of theirs inherit those eyes the way Laura had? Just the thought of carrying Ben's child was enough to turn her knees to water, and as for thinking about the pleasure the two of them would give each other as they put that child there…

'Of course I love you,' she said softly, taking that final step that put her in his arms. 'And it doesn't matter what you're called or what job you want to do, as long as you love me and we can be a family.'

'Oh, Kat!' He swept her off her feet and swung her round in a dizzying circle of celebration, before bending his head to take her lips in a kiss that left her in no doubt about his feelings.

'Marry me *soon*,' he demanded, when they came up for air several breathless minutes later. 'We can't take any chances with three chaperons in the house, and I don't want to wait any longer than we have to before we're sharing a bed.'

'Soon,' she agreed, as she slid her fingers through the thick dark hair at the back of his head to pull him back to her, her mouth already tingling with anticipation. 'But in the meantime…'

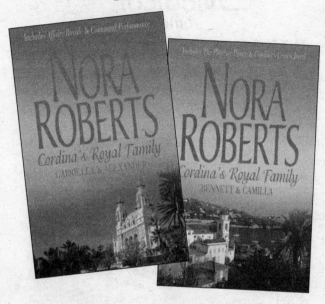

FREE

4 BOOKS AND A SURPRISE GIFT!

We would like to take this opportunity to thank you for reading this Mills & Boon® book by offering you the chance to take FOUR more specially selected titles from the Medical Romance™ series absolutely FREE! We're also making this offer to introduce you to the benefits of the Mills & Boon® Reader Service™—

- ★ **FREE home delivery**
- ★ **FREE gifts and competitions**
- ★ **FREE monthly Newsletter**
- ★ **Books available before they're in the shops**
- ★ **Exclusive Reader Service offers**

Accepting these FREE books and gift places you under no obligation to buy; you may cancel at any time, even after receiving your free shipment. Simply complete your details below and return the entire page to the address below. You don't even need a stamp!

YES! Please send me 4 free Medical Romance books and a surprise gift. I understand that unless you hear from me, I will receive 6 superb new titles every month for just £2.80 each, postage and packing free. I am under no obligation to purchase any books and may cancel my subscription at any time. The free books and gift will be mine to keep in any case.

M7ZEE

Ms/Mrs/Miss/Mr......................................Initials ....
BLOCK CAPITALS PLEASE

Surname ....

Address ....

....

....Postcode ....

Send this whole page to:
The Reader Service, FREEPOST CN81, Croydon, CR9 3WZ